For: Connie Brandley

With much love and happy memories of N.C.H.F.

Noellene Moore
10-12-96

To my sister, Nettie Johnson Hult,
without whose encouragement,
editorial skills, and expertise
this story could not have been written.

Chapter One

☾

In May of 1865, a small band of Confederate cavalrymen rode south through middle Georgia. The strong cavalry horses were being pushed almost beyond their endurance, but the mission of these soldiers demanded speed. They were trying to get the Confederate gold in their possession as far away from the pursuing Yankees as humanly possible.

Jefferson Davis, President of the Confederate States of America, had been captured near the small town of Irwinsville, Georgia. He had hoped to reach Florida and from there proceed to General Kirby Smith's outfit in Texas. If that plan failed, he had then hoped to make his way safely to Mexico. He had caught up with his wife, Varena, their family, and her entourage as they traveled south. His main objective had been to evade the Yankee soldiers and assure the safety of his family. His escape, however, had been cut off when he was recognized while camped near Irwinsville.

The cavalrymen who were carrying a portion of the Confederate gold realized that the South's hopes were gone with the capture of their president. The Confederacy was dead. The South, especially Georgia, had been devastated. These men hoped some day to return to their respective homes, but first they had to dispose of the gold in their possession. Confederate paper currency would likely be worth nothing now, but gold was gold—no matter where it was found. They had to find a hiding place for this treasure—any place to keep it out of the hands of those northern soldiers who had torn up their homeland. Many of these men were from Georgia, and the devastation they had witnessed as they rode through their state made their blood boil. They must ride, ride, even if the horses dropped.

Under cover of a thick clump of trees, the captain raised his hand for a sudden halt. This was the first chance he had had to talk with his men since the mad escape began. He motioned for his men to dismount and gather around him.

"We are on a wild ride, soldiers. We must keep this gold out of the hands of the enemy. Those damn Yankees have sapped the very life's blood from our southland. The Confederacy is gone, and this gold now belongs to no one. President Davis hoped to get to Texas and meet with General Kirby Smith, but since he is in the hands of the Federals, there is no hope of carrying on. It's just a matter of time before General Smith and the other Confederate generals must capitulate. Even if we could get the gold to Texas, the Federals would only confiscate it when our troops there fall to the Yankees. Now, we can either divide this gold among ourselves, or we can find a safe hiding place for it. I have a friend who has a plantation just across the Georgia line, in Madison, Florida. We're not too far from there. We can hide it there and get it off our hands. That I am anxious to do. If the Federals catch up with us, somebody will get killed, because I am giving nothing to those Yankees without a fight. So, what do you want to do with it?"

"Head for Madison," one soldier said.

"Let's divide it here and now," suggested another.

At that point, Corporal Sim Ross spoke up. "Well, Sir, if you all don't mind, I want to go home. I don't want none o' that Confederate gold. I've saved most of my pay these war years, and now it ain't no good. I got a big roll of Confederate money over there in my saddlebag. I guess I can use it to paper the walls of our house in the

Okefenok. All I want is to get on home to my folks. If you'll just muster me out, I'll be on my way south and into my native swamp land."

"We all want to go home, Sim, but we must take care of this gold. Look, just take your share and go on home. You don't have too far to ride now from here."

"I surely do not want none o' that gold on my hands, Captain. With your permission, I'll just tell you all goodbye and head for the swamps."

Before the captain would dismiss him, he took one of the older sergeants aside and spoke with him in a subdued tone. Afterward, the sergeant walked over to Sim's horse and loaded his saddlebag with what looked like sacks of food for Sim's ride home.

Sim said his goodbyes, thanked his captain for releasing him, mounted his big Confederate horse, and headed south. He did not want any of the gold, yet he held no qualms about riding off on a horse marked CSA. This horse had been such a major part of his life for so long that anyone would have had a rough time separating him from the animal.

As he rode south, Sim wondered how everything was at home, if Ma and Pa were well, if they had changed much during the four years that he had been away. He wondered especially if his girl, Minnie Lou, was still single. She had been sixteen when he left, but four years would now make her a young woman of twenty. Had she forgotten him? Had she married someone else? Well, he would soon know.

After riding hard for several hours, Sim decided to stop and see what food he had left in his saddlebag. He found that the sergeant had indeed left him some food, but there was something else in the saddlebag as well. Whatever it was seemed heavy, and Sim knew he had to travel with a light load. As he tried to lift the bag out, he found it so heavy that he had to use both hands.

"What th' hell? That rascal sergeant's done played a trick on me," he said to himself. He dropped the bag to the ground and told himself that if he ever saw that rascal again, he would get even with him.

He slowly opened the bag, and suddenly the sunshine revealed its contents: pure, shining gold.

Sim was so shocked that he stepped back. After a moment, he eased up and touched the gold. He realized what the captain must have ordered the sergeant to do. This was Sim's share of the gold. He had no idea what it was worth. He didn't care, and he certainly didn't want it. If those Feds caught up with him, he would be put in jail for years. Maybe they'd even shoot him.

He tried to eat his meager rations, but his appetite had gone. What was he to do with this unwanted treasure? He was riding a horse that obviously belonged to the Confederacy. He was wearing a Confederate uniform and had no civilian clothes. He knew there was no way to get the gold back to his outfit. He didn't know where they now were, and he had no idea where Madison, Florida was. Besides, from the presence of the gold in his saddlebag, it seemed likely that they had changed their minds and decided to divide up the gold instead of taking it on to Madison.

"This is a hell of a mess," Sim said to himself. "I ain't no thief. I'm a proud soldier of the Confederacy and will be till the day I die. I ain't never been a coward, and I ain't one now. I'll just pack up this mess o' gold, keep my gun handy, and shoot whoever tries to stop me. I'm goin' home to Ma and Pa and to Min, if she still wants me."

He knew, however, that he must get out of his Confederate uniform, but he thought it best to stay away from the little towns on the way. To get home, he would have to skirt the east side of the swamp for some distance and enter from the southeast. Surely he could stop at some farm house and buy some old clothes to disguise his recent position in the Confederate army. Surely these country people were loyal southerners. He would just have to take his chance at the next farm house.

It had not yet dawned on Sim that he was carrying a treasure that could make him a rich man. All he knew was that he had something in his possession that he did not want—something that he was hell bent on keeping out of the hands of the Yankees, the bloody bastards who had killed so many of his friends. He could see them now, lying in the snow turned red by their life's blood flowing from them. The more he thought about it, the madder he got, and the faster he rode.

Suddenly, in the distance, he saw a nice-looking farm house. Wet laundry flapped in the wind on the clothesline behind the house, so someone had to be there. Suppose they were Yankee sympathizers? That, however, was a chance he must take, so he rode slowly up the path to the house.

An elderly man and woman came out to meet him, anxiety written on their wrinkled faces. For a moment, when they saw the Confederate uniform, they thought it might be the son they had not heard from in over three years.

"Are you from the Confederate Army? Have you any news of our boy, Dave Cates? He's been gone for three years now," the man said.

Sim knew he was on safe ground now. If their son was a rebel, they would welcome him and any news he had.

"No, sir, I don't know your boy, but he may be comin' home soon, as the war is mostly over. President Davis has been captured, and there's no use to go on fightin'. I've been mustered out by my captain, so I'm free to go home, but I need your help. Can I trust you to help me escape any Yankee soldiers who may be followin' me?"

"I'll blow any Yankee I see to hell," the man answered as he and his wife each grabbed the guns that were anchored outside the front door.

"Now, I don't know for sure that they are followin' me, but as you can see, I have kept my army horse. Them damn Yankees may try to take him from me, and I have to have him to get home. My folks live in the south swamp, down near the St. Marys River. If you have some old clothes that you can sell me, I'll get out of this uniform. Then, maybe I can fool them if they catch up with me. I don't know what to do about the CSA brand on the horse, but I'll think of somethin'."

"You go on inside, Son. I'll take care of the horse, and Ma will get you some of our boy's old clothes. I have a branding iron that I use on my cattle. I'll fix that brand to where nobody can recognize it."

Sim followed the woman inside. Not only did she get him some of her son's old clothes, but she also prepared him a good, hot meal.

Sim was tired. The day had been hard for him, and he was still a long way from home. It did not take much urging for him to accept their invitation to stay on for the night. Even though it was too early for a normal bedtime, Sim was soon settled in their boy's room. How long had it been since he had slept in a real bed? Humble though it was, this room was like heaven to him. Before he fell asleep, he thanked God for these good people and prayed that their son would get back home safe and sound. He especially prayed that Ma, Pa, and Min would still be in the south swamp when he got there.

He was in no hurry to leave the next morning. He lingered over a good, hot breakfast and tried to answer the many questions these anxious parents asked about the war. They hung on his every word, and he could understand their anxiety. Knowing that his own parents were likely having the same worries, he finally bade them goodbye and headed for the south swamp.

As he rode south, he could hardly believe that he had finally been released from the army and was returning to the quiet, rural life that he had left four years ago. What would become of the South now? The war was lost, and the Confederacy would crumble. He had seen only the eastern section of Georgia as he had ridden south with the cavalry, but he had heard of the devastation left by Sherman's army as they burned Atlanta and captured Savannah. How could any decent human punish women and children as Sherman's army had? There was no telling how much additional punishment would be inflicted on the South as the Federals heaped their hatred on their former enemies. Well, one thing was for sure: if he could make it safely home, no one would ever find him there.

As he considered his future and that of Georgia and the South in general, the thought of that damned gold hit him anew. He did not want it; he did not need it. What little he needed could be purchased with money from the sale of a few farm products or a small amount of timber. Also, there were the stills that Pa had set up deep in the swamp. He wondered if Pa still hauled spirits down to Florida like he did when Sim left. Those folks at Jacksonville would buy any amount you could haul down. So what did he need with Confederate gold? It was just something to worry him and to make him afraid that the Federal soldiers would be after him.

Sim had heard all kinds of rumors about members of the confederacy. Some said that Judah P. Benjamin, a member of the president's cabinet for four years and his right-hand man, had taken a large sum of gold and headed for Florida. Of course, Benjamin was a rich man in his own right, but now the Federal troops were after him. Sim hoped that Benjamin would escape and perhaps get away to England or some other foreign country. He knew that other important Confederates were trying to escape the Federals. Maybe they would move out west and hopefully be safe. But here he was, a south Georgia swamp boy who had fought for his beloved southland, and he was probably being pursued like a common criminal. How he wished that sergeant had not thrust that gold upon him! Sim understood that the captain had thought he was doing the right thing, but he just did not know how much agony and trouble his action would cause Sim.

Sim had thought he was a man now, a man who had fought and seen men fight and die for the Confederacy. Now, however, he found himself feeling like a boy again, wanting to ask his Ma and Pa for advice. The feeling comforted him, however, because he knew that Pa would know what to do with the gold. That was it—Pa would know. Relieved, Sim spurred his horse to go a little faster toward the safety of his parents and the beautiful Okefenokee.

Finally, he could see Traders Hill in the distance. He considered riding into the town but soon thought better of it. He had heard that there were Federals all along the east coast. Since this was the main trading center of the area, there were probably northern soldiers around. He skirted the little town and rode on toward the south swamp. For a moment, he considered going around the southeast end of the swamp and riding in along the St. Marys River, but then he recalled a shorter route. It would be a little more difficult for his horse, but since there seemed to have been a dry spell, he decided to take the chance of entering on the east a little distance below Traders Hill. If the water became too much for his horse, he could always turn back.

"Okay, Bob," he said to his horse, "you ain't never seen such beauty as I'm gonna show you, but the goin' won't be easy. Just keep your footin', and I'll keep off any varmints that may come after us.

"You'll like Ma and Pa, Bob, and they'll like you. You can be lots of help to us on the little farm. I'm real proud of you, Bob, and I promise to take good care of you. I know you come from that high class area in Virginia, but we're good folks, too. You'll get used to our ways. Now, I'll tell you a little more 'bout Ma and Pa. They came down from Carolina a long time ago. I think they came down here because Pa actually stole his girl from another man. Her Pa wanted her to marry some old man who had a big farm, but she didn't love him, you see. Since she loved Pa, they slipped away one night and headed for Georgia. Just to be on the safe side, they settled in the south swamp. They still love each other, and they say they have never been sorry. They got married in a little town just across the Georgia line. They had the preacher who married them to write to her Pa so he would know that they did the right thing and got married. I'm glad they did that, 'cause I know that poor old man was worried 'bout his girl. Her name was Agatha McCall, but folks call her 'Miss Aggie.' Pa's name is James Simpson Ross. Swamp people call him 'Mr. Jim.'"

Sim felt that Bob partly understood what he was saying. He seemed to be doing all he could to get Sim safely to the little Ross farm over near the big lake.

"You and me, Bob, we're gonna make life easier for Ma and Pa. They're gettin' older, but we're young and strong. Oh, I forgot to tell you about Min. Her name is Minnie Lou Price, and she is real pretty. At least, she was when I left for the army. If she's up and married somebody else, I'll sure be disappointed. Well, we'll soon find out, Bob. Just keep your footin' and don't pay any attention to these varmints we're meetin'. Now, that bear over there may be a problem. If he starts at us, don't you worry, 'cause I'll shoot him. But I don't want to if I don't have to, 'cause I've had enough shootin' to last me a long time."

Sim did not have to shoot the bear because it made a quick escape to the woods. For the first time in a very long while, Sim heard the noises of the swamp—noises he had heard all his life: the chirping of birds, the screeching of wood owls, the groan of alligators, and the grunts of hoards of frogs. How beautiful the sounds were compared to the blasting of guns and cannons, to the cries of wounded and dying men. Even the famous "rebel yell" no longer made his heart beat faster. There was one yell, however, that he must soon put into use: the swamp holler. Many times he had shown his buddies this holler, but none were ever able to master it. Only a real swamper knew how to make the holler that could carry well over two miles. Before too long he would make this call. He only hoped that there would be an answering holler from Ma and Pa as he approached his home in the south swamp.

Sim was beginning to get tired. His horse was having a rough time crunching through the mushy, watery land.

"Now, Bob, don't give up," he told his horse. "I know you're tired, but so am I. We sure can't stop here, so we have to get home before dark."

Bob seemed to understand, and he struggled on. The shadows were closing in on them, but Sim thought he recognized some small landmarks, which meant that they were nearing his home.

"Oh, please, God, let Ma and Pa be there," he prayed. With that, he made the standard swamp holler. He heard no response, so he let out another holler. This time he got a response. Faint as it was, he knew it was Pa. There was no mistaking Pa's special holler. Then— thanks be—he heard another holler, one that was more shrill, one that was definitely from Ma. He continued to sound his greeting, and the welcoming greetings got stronger and stronger. As Sim and Bob lurched faster and faster toward the sounds, Sim suddenly saw two figures running toward him, lanterns held over their heads and screams of delight coming forth.

"Oh, Sim, Sim you're back!" Ma yelled. "Praise God, you're back!"

"Are you all right, boy? Is the war over, Son?" called Pa.

"Yeah, Ma, I'm back, and I'm all right. Yeah, Pa, the war is 'bout over now. I'm back for good. The war is lost, but I'm home at last."

Sim slid to the ground and ran toward his parents' outstretched arms. Bob stood quietly, as though he were a statue.

When Ma finally stopped crying, Sim turned toward Bob and took the dangling bridle in his hands. "Now, this here is my horse, Bob. His real name is Robert E. Lee, but I call him Bob for short. He's a fine Virginia horse. I kept him when I was discharged, but I'll tell you all 'bout that later. We'd better get out of these woods before it's black dark."

Sim put his arms around his parents again, and they walked toward home. Bob followed without being told to do so. Evidently he wanted to get some food and fresh water. Bob was tired, very tired. These last two days had been almost too much, even for a strong Confederate horse.

Pa took charge of Bob after Sim had unloaded his gear. He knew the horse needed food and water. He ran their two oxen from the barn and made a place there for Bob. In the meantime, Sim unpacked his belongings and got settled in his old room while Ma started a fire in the kitchen stove. She began to prepare her boy a supper of ham, eggs, and fresh grits. There were biscuits left over from their early supper that she would warm in a short while. Sim went to the back porch where a water bucket and wash pan stood ready to accommodate him. He took only a short time to clean up from his long ride because the smell of that sizzling ham was luring him back to Ma's kitchen.

Just as Sim took his seat at the kitchen table, Pa came in and announced that Bob was watered, fed, and comfortably situated. Ma and Pa drank coffee with Sim as he dove into the good food. Ma was so happy that she kept dabbing at the tears that would not stop. Her boy was home, her only child whom she had feared would never return. She had wondered many times if he had fallen on some battlefield, and she had been afraid that she and Pa would reach old age and die alone in the south swamp.

When Sim finally slowed down a bit in his eating, he relaxed and began to talk to his parents. "Now, you all may not know it, but the war is lost. President Davis has been captured up near Irwinsville.

He was tryin' to get to Texas. I don't know what they will do with him, but the Confederate capital at Richmond is in the hands of the Yankees—most of the rest of the South is, too. They have burned Atlanta and captured Savannah. But don't think I'm runnin' away. I was a good, loyal soldier. But when I saw that the South was gone, I asked my captain to discharge me, and he did. I've got the paper that he signed to let me go, so you need not worry that I'm home when I should not be here, or that I'm runnin' away.

"I've got a big roll of Confederate money 'cause I saved most of my pay these past years, but it's not likely any good now. I'll show it to you after 'while. I've got something else to show you, too, but first I want to check these doors and windows to be sure nobody's peekin' in, not even one o' them Indians who live around here."

With that, he got up from the table, checked all the windows and doors, and went back to his room for the roll of paper currency and the bag of unwanted gold. Ma and Pa did not know what to make of it; they thought he was acting peculiarly. What could he be afraid of at this point? Was someone after him?

As Sim settled back in his kitchen chair, he took out the big roll of paper currency and put it on the table. His parents gasped at what they saw. Surely this could not be worthless! But Sim again told them that most likely it was no good now. He then took out the bag of gold and placed it on the table.

"Good heavens, boy! You ain't turned to robbery, have you?"

"No, Pa. I'm gonna tell you all 'bout this gold, but you must never mention it to a person on this earth. Understand?"

They promised him that they would do whatever he wished, but they were still puzzled. Sim assured his parents that he had not stolen the gold and proceeded to explain how it came into his possession.

"To run a gov'ment, you know, the president and the people who help him need lots o' money. When President Davis saw that the Yankees were gonna take over Richmond, he had the money in the Confederate treasury shipped south. Most of this money was in gold bullion—bars—but some of it was molded into coins. The Yankees took over most of the bullion at Augusta and shipped it up to Washington. But the Confederate soldiers got away with some of it, and some of the gold coins, too. A good deal of it was captured along with President Davis, but our outfit got away with as much as we could, and this is a small part of what was left of them gold coins.

"But, you see, when President Davis was captured, there was no hope that the Confederacy would live on. All was lost. That's when I asked my captain to let me out of the army. He offered me some of the gold that our unit had managed to get away with, but I just told him I didn't want it. All I wanted was to get on home to my people. Well, he signed my paper to let me out. I told all o' my buddies goodbye and headed for home.

"That ain't the end o' the story, though. While I was gettin' my paper signed, I saw the captain say something to a sergeant, and the sergeant went over and put something in my saddlebag. I thought it was some rations for me to have on the road, but on my way down, I found this here sack o' gold that he had put in my saddlebag along with some food. I guess the captain figured it was my part o' the gold. I don't know just how much it is, but I don't want it. We can make our own livin' down here. I would have carried it back to the outfit, but I didn't know where they were. As a matter of fact, I don't know what happened to the rest of the outfit at all. I guess they headed either for Texas or Mexico, or maybe divided the gold and went on home. So there was nothing else I could do but head on home, too. Did I do the right thing, Pa?"

"O' course you did, Sim. There wasn't nothin' else you could have done. Do you think the Yankees will try to get it?"

"That's why I say not to mention it to anybody. There's Yankee soldiers over around St. Marys and up and down the coast, and there's no tellin' where else. They might accuse me of stealing and put me in a federal prison. So, what do I do with this gold? Ma, you ain't said nothin'. What do you think?"

"If you want my opinion, Son, I say to hide it," answered Ma. "Them Yankees can't stay in Georgia forever. Some day you'll have a family of your own, and if I judge right, that's a nice bit o' money to help raise a family. That reminds me, you ain't asked about Minnie Lou. I hope you ain't found another girl up where you've been."

"I've been puttin' that question off 'cause I was so afraid that she had married somebody else. Is she still single? Do you all ever get to see her?"

"Yeah, she's waitin' for you to get back, and we see her when we get down to Bethel Church," Ma answered. "She has made a real pretty woman. She'll be awfully glad to know you're back home."

Sim's heart skipped a beat. Min was still single and waiting for him! What more could he ask from life? His parents had been waiting for him, and now his girl, Min. He would soon get his life back together, but first he must attend to that gold. Pa's voice brought his thoughts back to the situation at hand.

"Your Ma is right, boy. Let's hide that gold for the time bein'—maybe even for a few years. Gold lasts forever, so at some proper time you can get a trusty banker to handle it for you. I hope that when that time comes, you'll see fit to buy land with it. These swamps of ours are a real gold mine. This small plot that we own ain't worth much right now, but when the country settles down from the war, folks will see the worth of these trees and the animals that live amongst 'em. It may take a long time for everything to settle back to normal, but that day will come.

"Another bit of advice I will give you, even though you may not see fit to take it, is that you not even mention this to Minnie Lou. I know that she is a fine Christian girl, but right now I don't think I'd trust anybody."

Ma agreed to this, and since Sim felt that his parents were wiser than he was, he decided to take their advice. Anyway, he had not seen Min in a very long time. There was no telling how much she might have changed.

They decided to bury the gold out behind the barn. Ma had a sturdy metal box where she kept her special possessions, and she volunteered to empty it and let it serve to hold the gold. Sim took the chance of leaving the treasure in the house for one night, but early the next morning he and Pa dug a hole at the assigned spot behind the barn. As soon as the box of gold was well into the ground and the swamp dirt was piled on top, they planted a fast-growing shrub over the spot. Sim felt a great sense of relief. He could now enjoy his parents' company and make plans to pay a visit to Minnie Lou.

To get to the island where Min's family lived, Sim would have to go by boat. Pa had a couple of good boats and plenty of poles and paddles that could be used to maneuver through the vine-entangled swamp water. Sim knew the trip would take several hours, so on his third day at home, he took the lunch Ma had prepared for him and set out just after sun-up. The smell of the early morning swamp and the sounds of the birds, frogs, and alligators were enough to lift his spirits. He could almost forget the war for a while. Since he had returned home, he was finding it harder to forget than he realized. There were too many flashbacks to death and injury on the battlefield. He had talked to his parents about these memories, and they assured him that time would heal most of his worries.

Ma had wisely taken his uniform, washed it, and put it in a safe place. He had managed to keep a Confederate flag from a major battle where the South had been victorious. Ma also washed and carefully put this flag away. Sim was thinking of these things as he poled his way across the big lake, until suddenly a huge alligator appeared in the distance. Sim was not afraid. He knew how to maneuver around the big reptile, but he was surprised to realize that he had forgotten how ugly the creatures were.

"Get outta my way, you old oversized lizard," he shouted. That made him feel better, and he poled his way away from the creature and hoped no others would get in his way.

The water lilies were in full bloom, and the lakes were dotted with green and white as far as he could see. He was so much involved in the beauty around him that he almost went up the wrong run, which was a canal-like waterway. Many people could get lost in that area, but not Sim. This was his territory, had been all of his life, and no amount of time away from home could dull his sense of direction here.

The sun was getting high in the sky now, and Sim was beginning to feel anxious about what he would encounter when he reached the

Price's island home. Minnie Lou's brothers, Jake and Caleb, had evaded the Confederate draft. Sim's parents had told him how the two young men had literally hidden out to keep from going into the army. Sim did not care that they had dodged military service. Ma and Pa said that quite a few young men had hidden out in the swamp area to keep from fighting. All Sim cared about was that he had done his part for the Confederacy. He was proud that he was not afraid to serve, but if those other Georgians were not willing to fight, so be it. They had a right to their beliefs. He knew that some people might call them cowards, but all Sim cared about was that he was a brave soldier and was willing to fight for what he believed. He hoped that Jake and Caleb would not shy away from him because he had been a Confederate soldier. They had to live with their conscience; his was clear because he had done what he thought was right. He supposed that they had done what they believed was right, too.

Sim was so deep in his own thoughts that he had reached the run that led to the Price home before he realized it. He lifted his pole into the boat and let out a loud, clear holler. He waited a few minutes and let forth another good swamp holler. He listened, and there it was—loud and clear. It was Min's special holler. She had recognized his voice. Sim's heart began to beat faster, and he grabbed up his pole and headed down the run. In a short while, he could see Min standing on the edge of the big pond that went almost up to the Price house. She was waving and shouting, but Sim was still too far away to hear her words clearly. Finally, he poled his boat to the landing, jumped out, and took Min in his arms. The rest of the family gathered around them, and Min and her mother were both crying. Mr. Price and the boys were all offering to shake hands. Sim noticed that Jake and Caleb were very quiet, but all the others were talking at one time.

"Are you home for good, Sim?" asked Min.

"Are you well? Are you through with all the fightin'?" asked Min's Pa.

Sim's answer to the affirmative brought warm smiles to all. With one arm around Min and one around her Ma, he joined the others as they headed toward the house.

"It's been so long, Son. We thought you'd never get back," said Ma Price. "Will that war ever be over? Down here in the swamps, we don't get much news of what's goin' on. My two boys here, Jake and Caleb, were 'bout ready to go over to St. Marys and join up, but I kept tellin' 'em to wait and find out how things were goin'."

"It's best, I guess, that they didn't join up," said Sim. "You all needed them here to help around the place. Besides, the war is practically over now."

Sim saw relief on Jake's and Caleb's young faces. He then told them about the capture of President Davis, the burning of Atlanta, and the capture of Savannah. This was all news to them. Swamp people minded their own business and let the rest of the world do the same. With Sim home, however, they suddenly had a source of news, and they flooded him with questions.

There was so much family talk that Sim and Min had almost no time for personal talk. Sim could only feast his eyes on Min's lovely face, her deep blue eyes, and her golden hair. Somehow he had to find time to talk with Min away from her doting family. Ma Price saved the day finally by ordering the men folks to their chores and the younger girls to the kitchen to help prepare dinner. She left Sim and Min on the front porch to do their personal talking.

Left alone with Min after four long years of separation, Sim felt suddenly shy and tongue-tied. He turned to talk of the weather and crops and moonshining.

"Sim, aren't you glad to see me?" asked Min. "Who cares about weather and such? I'm so glad to see you, I feel that I could burst with joy! Did you find another girl when you were in the army? If you did, please just tell me about her."

"Good heavens, Min, I would never have another girl! Now that I'm here, it's just that I don't know what to say. I know what I feel, but I can't seem to say it."

"Okay, Sim Ross, I'll help you. Do you still love me like you did when you went down to St. Marys and joined the army?"

"Oh, Min, I love you a thousand times more." His shyness left him, and he continued. "During those long nights in the army, I thought of you back here in the south swamp. I wanted to be with you, and I prayed you'd wait for me until the war was over. I just can't believe my prayers have actually been answered. So I'll just ask you now: will you marry me?"

Min started crying but still managed to give him a clear "yes." Ma was calling dinner then, so the remainder of their conversation would have to wait. Sim did get up the nerve by the end of the meal to ask Min's parents for permission to marry her. His request was no surprise to them, and they readily gave their consent.

The world seemed right once more. Well before dark, Sim left for home after promising to meet Min and her family the following Sunday at Bethel Church, the Primitive Baptist church near Moniac, which both families attended.

Chapter Two

☾

As planned, both families attended the Bethel Church on the following Sunday. Sim's parents were extremely pleased with his plans to marry Min, and Min's family seemed just as happy. After the dinner on the grounds, the two families got together, away from the crowd, to discuss plans for the upcoming wedding. Sim and his Pa had already decided to enlarge Sim's room to make a more comfortable place for Sim and Min to start their life together. Some day they might build a new house on the Ross island, but most likely they would just build on to the homeplace as the need arose. At any rate, Sim would always be close by to help with the family farming, the tending of stock, and the operation of the family stills.

Min's pa, Zeke Price, and her brothers insisted that they go over to the Ross place to help with the room enlargement. This was the way of the swamp people, and Sim knew that other church friends would help if they were needed.

Following the afternoon sermon, both families headed for home with plans to begin cutting the timber that would be needed for the new construction. Min wanted to go along with the men, but her mother insisted that she remain at home so that they could get started on some wedding clothes.

By late afternoon, each family was well on its way home. They had made arrangements with the preacher to perform the wedding in one month. All of the church members were invited, and these friends immediately began making plans for the wedding feast to be held on the church grounds following the ceremony.

As Sim poled through the swamp waters with Ma and Pa at his side, he could hardly believe that in such a short time he had settled back into the routine of swamp life and had begun to put the past four years behind him. As he viewed the beauty around him and listened to the peaceful noises of the swamp, he let his mind wander back, as it did so often now, to the army experiences he had left behind. The sudden call of a swamp bird brought tears to his eyes; for a moment, it sounded like his old buddy, Jim Brown, who had called to him when he was shot. Sim had rushed to Jim's side, but it had been too late.

Ma saw the tears and asked Sim if something was wrong. "Aren't you happy about the weddin', Son?"

"Oh, yes, Ma. I've been hoping for this for a long time. I was just remembering my friend Jim who died at Manassas. That bird call sounded just like his voice."

Ma assured Sim that she understood and that time would take away some of the hurt. She herself often remembered the sad and agonizing times back home during the Carolina mountain feuds. She had seen death and suffering when trouble had broken out between her family and a nearby clan.

Sim's spirits lifted as their house came into view, and he remembered that Min would soon be part of that home. He could see his faithful Bob peering over the fence around the barn, as if to ask where they had been and why they had been gone so long.

Ma reminded Sim that he needed new clothes. She had noticed how skimpy his suit had looked when they were at church. Not only had Sim's young body filled out, but the years he had been gone had also taken a toll on his clothes. Ma had preserved them the best she could, but even that had not been enough. Besides, she wanted her boy to be the most handsome man at the wedding.

"I think I can ride Bob over to Traders Hill by cuttin' through the marsh," said Sim. "Pa, do you think the dry spell has cleared the area out enough for Bob to get through?"

"It's all right if you stay to the south of the main marsh. I drove the ox cart down that way not too long ago. I didn't go all the way to Traders Hill, but I did go as far as the river. I was sending some spirits to St. Marys. We've got a friend living down on the river, and he takes any amount of spirits we can make. But we still send a lot of it down to Florida.

"Be careful, boy, how you dress to go to Traders Hill," Pa advised. "Look as old as you can, 'cause I heard that them damn Yankee soldiers are thick as flies over there still."

Sim kept his father's advice in mind as he dressed for his trip. He would attempt to ride Bob, but if the land was too boggy, he would turn back and take one of the boats down as far as he could go. After that, it would be necessary to walk the rest of the way. But that didn't worry Sim too much. After all, he had walked many miles in the army. Besides, there was always someone out in a wagon or cart of some kind. These good country folk were not likely to pass by without offering someone a ride.

Ma had saved some money from the produce they sold to people in the little towns, and she gave it to Sim for his trip. Just for good measure, he took along some of his Confederate money. He doubted that he could buy anything with it, but perhaps the people over at Traders Hill did not know yet that it was completely worthless. He thought it was worth a try. If it worked, he would buy Ma material for a new dress and a new suit for Pa. He also had a secret hope that he would be able to buy a ring for Min. If not today, he knew that some day he would buy her a gold wedding band. It would mean so much more to her, though, if she could have it for her wedding day. Maybe the money was not as worthless as he had thought, or maybe the Washington government would cover the Confederate money. Well, it wouldn't hurt to try.

In his old, worn-out clothes and a slouch hat that covered his head and most of his face, he set out for Traders Hill. There might be some folks that he knew in town, but he would try to avoid them for now.

Sim reached Traders Hill well before noon and carefully scanned the town. He left Bob hidden outside because a strong, well-fed horse would attract too much attention. People in the South were hungry, and the animals which had not been confiscated by the Federals were thin and emaciated. Sim knew that there was a chance that Bob could be stolen, so he found a thick area of trees and tied his horse securely.

Sim did not actually expect anyone to recognize him. He had grown a short beard, and he hardly recognized himself when he looked in the mirror. He would be going over to see Min in a few days, and he would ask her if she wanted him to shave before the wedding.

As he worked his way through the small town, he realized how run-down everything looked. The stores had very little to offer, and the people were shabbily dressed. Most of them were either very old or very young. He remembered Traders Hill as a bubbling, happy little town, but no one seemed happy now. He did find a general store that had a few bolts of cloth and some inexpensive jewelry and trinkets. There were no men's clothes there, though, so he bought some cloth that he thought Ma would like and a ring for Min. The ring wasn't gold, but it was a fair grade of silver. The silver would do for now, but some day he would buy Min a beautiful gold ring. He had used Ma's money to buy these items, but he decided to try to use the Confederate money if he found a store with men's clothing.

He walked down the sandy street and found a store that did carry men's clothing. The man who ran the store was a real dyed-in-the-wool Yankee. His speech was so different from that of the southeast Georgians that it was difficult for Sim to understand him. After a short conversation with this man, Sim decided he wouldn't worry about the man losing money if he accepted the Confederate currency. After all, he should have stayed up North instead of coming down here to leach off these poor southerners. The price he asked for a suit was entirely too high. Sim was hesitant about dealing with the man, but when he realized that the Confederate currency was acceptable, he made the deal. The store owner was a little curious as to why this swamp man needed two nice suits, but thinking he had made a profitable deal, he kept his curiosity to himself.

Sim bought a crocus sack, put his purchases in the sack, and slung it over his shoulder. Anyone seeing him would think this poorly dressed swamp man had made household purchases and was planning to walk to his home somewhere deep in the swamp. That was the impression Sim hoped to make, since there were still a few Yankee soldiers walking up and down the streets.

He found Bob patiently waiting for him, and they started toward home. As Sim rode along, his thoughts turned to his plans to marry Min. He wondered if they would be happier living in one of the towns outside the swamp. There were jobs in the sawmills and even in the fishing industry down around St. Marys. He had not discussed any of this with Min, but he had already thought better of making such a move. Ma and Pa would never leave the swamp to live elsewhere, nor were Min's family likely to move to the outside, either. During those long years in the army, he had made no other plans than to return to the beautiful Okefenokee and some day live there with his own family.

Suddenly, as Sim mulled these things over again, he remembered that box of gold out behind the barn. When he finally put that treasure to use, would he and Min still be content to remain so isolated from the outside world? But he knew there was no way to answer that question now. Only time would solve that problem.

"Bob," Sim said, "I hope you are satisfied with your new home. I'm soon gonna have me a wife, and she'll love you like I do, 'cause you're such a good horse. If we ever have a child, Bob, you and I will teach that little person to ride. I don't expect you ever to be a work horse. You're too high-class for that. We'll let them oxen do the ploughing, won't we?"

As Sim talked, Bob picked up speed, and now they were moving along at a good pace on the dry land along the river trail. Soon, however, they would be crunching through the boggy area as they left the river and headed for the Ross place.

Sim felt that he had done some good trading that day. He had no qualms about using the Confederate currency to buy his and Pa's suits. If the store owner had been local, Sim would not have used the Confederate money. But that man was not from southeast Georgia, and the sooner he went back up North, the better. Sim realized that he was feeling prejudiced against his former enemy, but he couldn't help it. He had too many bad memories of those people. Perhaps some day he would be able to forgive them for what they had done to the South, especially to his native Georgia. But at least life in the swamp had changed very little in the past four years. The people still produced almost everything they needed, and until Sim could decide what to do with his gold, this quiet farm life in the swamp country would be enough for him. He only hoped it would be enough for Min. But it probably would be, because this was the only life she had ever known.

"Watch your step, boy," Sim cautioned Bob as he stumbled slightly. "We don't want a broken ankle."

They had reached marshy land, and the going would be slow the rest of the way. Sim was returning home, however, with a good feeling because he knew that Ma and Pa would be pleased with his purchases.

As Sim finally neared home, he let out a strong holler, which was promptly answered by Ma and Pa. They seemed anxious whenever he was out of their sight. He could understand their feeling, but if they only knew the dangers he had already faced in the past four years, they would realize how safe he was now.

Ma and Pa were like two children when they saw his sack full of purchases. Pa tried on his new suit, and it fit almost perfectly. Ma would do the few alterations that were needed. The same was true of Sim's new suit. Ma was already holding the new, bright pink floral material up in front of the small mirror that they possessed.

"Ma, you'll be so pretty in a dress made from that cloth. That's just the color you need," said Sim.

"Oh, I can't wait to make it up into a new dress, Son. There's enough material here for me to make a matching bonnet, too. You really did some good shoppin' today."

Sim told them about using the Confederate bills for the suits, and they both approved. In fact, Pa was already planning to go over to Traders Hill and unload some more of that Confederate money on the same store owner. He would wait a few days, however, until the men from the Price family came over to help build the new addition.

Sim showed Min's wedding ring to his parents, and they both liked it. But Ma reminded him that some day he would be able to buy her a real gold ring, maybe even one with a diamond in it, if he wanted to. Everything depended on what luck he would have with his buried treasure. When that subject came up, Pa again felt compelled to warn Sim to be cautious with his treasure.

"Don't be too hasty, Sim, about that gold. Whatever happens, I wouldn't touch it until all of them Yankee soldiers have cleared out of south Georgia. But don't worry, we've got several good stills goin'. Injun Joe and his family are tending them for me. They keep talkin' 'bout goin' to the Everglades in south Florida, but I'm hopin' they'll stay up here. They're good neighbors, and I know they're honest.

"There's a good market for our vegetables in the small settlements outside the swamp. Your Ma has had good luck with her chickens and eggs, too. With the Yankee gunboats ploughin' up and down the coast, goods have been scarce since it got so bad. Hides are selling real good, too. And Injun Joe keeps us in fish. That man can catch more fish than anybody I ever seen. So don't you worry about money or provisions. We'll have plenty for both families."

Sim assured Pa that he was not worried about provisions right now. What did worry him, though, was what he should do with the gold. Pa suggested again that he put the money in land. He knew it would buy hundreds of acres of good, timbered land, and people would need lumber for new houses and public buildings as they recovered from the war. The railroads would be extending their lines, too, and they would need cypress logs for crossties. Pa could see a very bright future for his son and Min, and hopefully for their children and grandchildren as well. But in the meantime, it was better to be content, mind their own business, and give help where it was needed.

Sim listened to his Pa's wise advice. When Pa suggested that it would be safer if he went himself to Traders Hill, Sim agreed. Pa was anxious to try his hand at spending more of the Confederate currency. Also, he was anxious to get to town and find out more about the end of the war. What would the Yankees do to the South now? Would the northern punishment reach into his beloved swamp land? Pa could ask such questions about the war now and be safer than someone who was young enough to have served in the Confederate army. Ma and Sim were in agreement. Pa would drive to Traders Hill in his homemade ox cart, which would attract less attention than a beautiful, healthy horse like Bob. As soon as the work on the room was underway, he would leave Sim in charge and head for Traders Hill.

Min's Pa, Mr. Zeke, and her two brothers, Jake and Caleb, soon came over to start work on the new room. With Mrs. Ross's permission, they would stay until the room was finished. She assured them that they were more than welcome, and she provided plenty of pallets for sleeping and ample food for all. In the meantime, Pa had gone to check on the stills and to tell Injun Joe about the building plans and Sim's upcoming marriage. Joe didn't know that Sim was back home; he had been in the north swamp helping to care for a sick brother. Joe's wife, Fawn, had taken good care of the stills while he was away, and she had also cared for their two children, six-year-old Dawn and four-year-old Pete.

When Fawn heard the good news, she volunteered to go and help Sim's mother cook for the men. Joe also volunteered his services to help with the building. "I will bring good spirits for the men to drink at night. It will make them sleep good after all the hard work."

These two Indians were good friends to Miss Aggie, as Sim's mother was called by the swamp people, and to Mr. Jim, as Pa was called. Pa knew that Joe would bring a good supply of fish, and Fawn would help Aggie feed the men each day. The Indian family—the Lightfoots—would return home each night and be back for work the following morning. The Lightfoot children were very happy to go over to see Miss Aggie and Mr. Jim. During the past four years, Dawn and Pete had been a source of joy for Aggie and Jim, as they waited and worried over what might happen to their only son, Sim. Now these children would finally get to meet the brave Confederate soldier about whom they had heard so much.

Aggie was very happy to hear that Fawn would be there to help her cook, and she was especially happy to know that little Dawn and Pete would be there for a nice visit. This building project was turning into a regular frolic! She regretted that Min and her Ma were not there to enjoy it with them, but she knew that they were busy getting Min's wedding clothes ready.

When the three Price men and the Indian family arrived soon after dawn the first morning, the men began cutting down trees and getting the logs ready for the building. The Prices even brought their own cross-cut saw and other tools, so the project progressed at a rapid rate. The food and nightly entertainment were so enjoyable that no one looked forward to the end of the work.

Everything was going so well that Mr. Jim decided to leave for Traders Hill. Sim peeled off a hundred Confederate dollars from his money roll and helped Pa hitch up the ox to the cart. Aggie prepared a nice lunch, and Jim was on his way before dawn. The marsh land was still dry enough that his little cart could get through without much trouble.

In addition to the Confederate money, he had a small amount of produce to trade. But this wouldn't buy much if the Confederate bills were no good. Well, he thought that it was worth the try. At least he could get over to Traders Hill and learn what he could about the war. Perhaps there would be news about what had actually happened since President Davis's capture. But, then again, maybe they didn't even know that President Davis had left Richmond. If they didn't, Jim certainly wouldn't tell them.

Jim Ross did a lot of thinking as he jostled along in his ox cart. Their life had been so quiet and peaceful since they had obtained a small plot of swamp land from a Headright Grant. The amount of land allotted to them had been small because the grant was based on the number of family members. At the time, there had been only two people in his family, himself and Aggie. Even when Sim came along, the land allotment had been sufficient and supplied plenty of dry land for farming. There were enough animals and fish to supply food and hides for marketing, so very little was needed from the outside. Their syrup, hides, chickens, eggs, and vegetables could be exchanged for medicine, tools, and farm equipment on the one or two trips a year that were necessary to the outside.

As Jim mused over the past, he wondered if he had always been fair to Aggie. She never complained, but very seldom had she gone to the outside with him when he went for supplies. She had seemed content with her swamp friends and the monthly trip to the Bethel Church near Moniac. Sim had helped to fill her life, and when he had gone away, she had suffered in silence. Jim knew, however, that she had lived in dread, just as he had, of bad news concerning their son and the outcome of the war.

Both Jim and Aggie had learned to read and write back in their youth in Carolina. In this respect, they were much better off than most of their neighbors. They had taught Sim to read and write, but few of his war letters had ever reached them because they were so isolated. They could, however, read the newspapers that Jim brought in from the outside. Sometimes they exchanged newspapers and news of the war with their friends at church. They had no way of knowing if these reports were true, but for those who had a family member in the service, any news was better than none at all. Jim and Aggie knew, however, that they had been lucky. Their boy had returned home, and he was now planning to marry a fine young girl.

Before he realized it, Jim had reached the outskirts of Traders Hill. He drove his cart into town and went first to the general store where he bartered his goods for supplies that Aggie had said they needed. After loading his supplies into the little ox cart, he went to the store where Sim had suggested he try to spend the Confederate money. This store was new to him. He had not been to Traders Hill for a long time, and it had been built since his last visit.

Jim looked around the store after greeting the owner, who had a strange way of speaking. There were some ready-made garments and many bolts of cloth. He knew Aggie could use some more material for dresses, shirts, and for curtains for the newly renovated room. He hoped he could get enough for Fawn and her family, too. They would love to have some new, colorful clothes, especially since material had been scarce for the past few years. Aggie's spinning wheel had helped, but homemade material was not as bright and colorful as the cloth that could be bought in the stores.

Jim realized that the material was overpriced. He spotted a nice mirror that would go well in the new room and found a ready-made shirt for Sim and some lace for Aggie's new dress. He added several cards of buttons, spotted some very pretty brooches, and added two of them to his list. He pointed out these articles to the storekeeper and asked what they cost. The merchant named a price well over what Jim knew it should be, but he bravely took out the bills and handed them over. Evidently the merchant had thought he would price him clearly out the door, and he was surprised when Jim gave him the money.

"I don't know if I should take any more Confederate money, Mister," he said. "You see, the war news is very bad for the South. There's a rumor that President Davis has fled Richmond and been captured. These soldiers here think the war may be over soon. In that case, this Confederate money won't be any good."

"Well, I sure as hell don't have no Yankee money, Mister, and I don't want none," replied Jim. "If you don't want my Confederate money, you can cram those goods down your throat for all I care." With that, Jim turned to walk out.

As he did so, the merchant thought better of the deal, called him back, and said, "I guess I might as well sell it to you as anybody else. The whole South is going to hell, anyway. As soon as I get rid of this merchandise, I'll be going back up North anyway. I sure can't take all this with me."

"Suit yourself," answered Jim, and he began carrying out the goods and loading them onto his cart. The two brooches he put into his shirt pocket.

A few minutes after he loaded up, he drove out of town. Afraid the merchant might change his mind and call him back, Jim pushed his ox cart along as fast as possible.

"Billy," he said to the ox, "we done pulled a fast one on that damn Yankee! Trot along as fast as you can. I can't wait to get home and show all my loot to Aggie and Sim! What we did is perfectly legal, so don't go thinkin' I'm a dishonest man. We've just done some good tradin', boy."

The shadows were beginning to lengthen as Jim and Billy reached the boggy edge of the swamp land, but Billy didn't mind. He had grown up in the swamp, and he had served the Ross family well. They had never overworked him, and his food had been the very best. He even got up a little trot as Jim urged him along.

Before black dark, Jim let out a good husky swamp holler and was answered by not one but several clear hollers from the Ross home. Aggie had put aside a good supper for Jim, and he ate while Sim and the Price boys unloaded the cart. Jim had even remembered to get a candy treat for all the workers and his family. Joe and his family had already gone home for the night, so their surprises would have to be delivered the next day.

After Jim ate his supper, the Price men, Sim, and Aggie gathered around to hear what news he had learned of the war. Jim joined the men in a little drink of spirits to ease his tired body. In the meantime, he asked Sim to move all the parcels from his shopping trip into his and Aggie's room. After receiving their candy treats and enjoying a little more spirits, the Prices retired to their pallets on the breezeway.

Aggie and Sim followed Jim into the bedroom to examine his purchases and to see if he had been able to use the Confederate money.

"I managed to spend some of it," he reported, "but that's probably the last we'll be able to use."

He handed the leftover bills to Sim. "Take these and put them with what you have left, Son. Maybe some day they'll be worth something, but right now I doubt it. Our part of the country is in a bad fix. It may not get any better for a while, but here in the swamp, folks will be able to get along. We can grow what we need, so there's no need to worry."

With that, he began opening packages. Aggie and Sim could not believe he had done such good trading. When Aggie saw all of the beautiful cloth and the lace, she was as happy as a little child. She said she would give the most colorful piece to Fawn and was already making plans to help her Indian friend make up the material into clothes for the Lightfoot family.

Sim's ready-made shirt was just right, and he tried it on so his parents could see how well it fit.

"Well, that's about it," said Jim. Then, with a grin, he reached into his shirt pocket. "Oh, I forgot this, Aggie. Here's a brooch I got for you from that damn Yankee. I got it with the Confederate money, so I guess we can call it your Confederate brooch."

"Oh, Jim, you are a sight," said Aggie. With tears running down her face, she tried to pin the brooch on her homemade gingham dress. "I know it don't go with this dress, but it will be so pretty on my new dress for the weddin'."

"Here, Ma," said Sim. "You can't pin it on with all them tears runnin' down your face. Let me do it."

He pinned the brooch on her dress and kissed her cheek. How he loved Ma and Pa!

Jim grinned from ear to ear, and as Sim started out the door, he said, "Wait a minute, Son, I forgot something else. Here's a brooch for my future daughter-in-law."

"Oh, Pa, I'll just have to go over to see her in a couple of days and give her this beautiful Confederate brooch. She'll be so happy."

Sim left them to go and get a good night's rest. Maybe another small sip of spirits would help him get to sleep so he could put in a good day's work tomorrow.

Chapter Three

☾

When the Lightfoot family received their gifts the morning after Jim's shopping spree, they were all thrilled. The candy prompted big hugs for Mr. Jim from Dawn and little Pete. Fawn was elated over the new, colorful material, and Joe Lightfoot thought he might even get a new shirt made from it. Aggie and Fawn teased him by promising to make him a fancy shirt for the wedding if he brought his whole family to the ceremony at Bethel Church. So Joe promised he would, and everyone was soon at work on their assigned duties.

After a couple of days, the work was going so well that Mr. Zeke thought he should go over for a few hours and check on the women in his family. When he asked Sim if he wanted to go along, Sim's face lit up so quickly that the others laughed and insisted that he go.

"Zeke probably needs some help rowin' and polin' through that plant-infested lake," suggested Mr. Jim, winking at Zeke.

"That's a good suggestion, Jim," he answered. "These heavy saws done got my shoulder muscles pretty sore. Do you mind goin' along, Sim?"

"Not at all, Sir," answered Sim. Of course he knew it was a setup, but he was glad to go anyway. He had been hoping to find some excuse to see Min and give her the Confederate brooch. Also, this trip would give him and Zeke a good chance to get to know each other better. He could talk personally with Min's Pa and assure him that he would take good care of his daughter. He wanted Mr. Zeke to know that he would work hard and try to give Min what she wanted and needed and would do his best to make her happy in her new home.

They found that Miss Ada, Min, and the two younger girls, Effie and Kate, were getting along fine. Min liked her brooch very much and was pleased to have a surprise visit from Sim. Zeke had saved his candy for his younger daughters, and Sim had brought his bag of candy for Miss Ada. Everyone was happy and assured Zeke that they were doing fine without him.

"Now, that gets me feelin' bad, ladies," Zeke teased. "Maybe I'll just stay over in the east swamp if you all don't need me."

"Oh, Zeke, you know what we meant," replied Miss Ada. "We just didn't want you and the boys to worry 'bout us."

"I know, Ada," said Zeke. "I was just funnin', but do be careful anyway. Keep them shotguns handy, but don't use 'em unless you have to. The work over there will be finished in a few days, and it's gonna be real pretty. Oh, Ada, I almost forgot. I brought you some spirits, just in case you need any for snakebites. One of you little girls run down to the boat and get it for your Ma."

"Well, if no snake comes along, I'll just use it for medicine. As a matter of fact, I may begin to feel poorly right away," laughed Ada.

Min noticed that Zeke had picked up his homemade banjo to take back with him. "Ma," she said, "I'm thinkin' that we're missin' some fun at the Ross place."

"You are, Min," answered Sim. "Every night we sit around on the porch after dark and pick and sing. Pa still plays his fiddle, and Ma has her banjo. We're lookin' forward to havin' your pretty voice join us, Min. There ain't never been a prettier voice than yours."

"Thank you, Sim, but don't forget that folks have always said you have the prettiest voice in the swamp."

"My army buddies used to ask me to sing for them when we sat around the camp fires, but it's been a long time since I could sing any of our old happy songs that we used to sing. Maybe now they'll come back to me."

Zeke announced that they had better leave if they wanted to get to the Ross place before dark. He kissed Miss Ada and the girls goodbye, and Sim did the same. With his arm around Min, Sim headed down to the boat. "Min, I hope you're as happy as I am about our marriage," he said.

"Oh, Sim, if you only knew how happy I am and how much I love you!" she exclaimed.

"I think I do, Honey, I think I do."

With that, he and Zeke got into the boat. Each picked up a pole, and they were soon out of sight among the green overhanging cypress limbs of the swamp.

"It's good to see my girl so happy, Sim," commented Zeke.

"She couldn't be half as happy as I am, Mr. Zeke. I've loved her for such a long time. I'm so thankful that she didn't marry somebody else while I was fightin' in the war."

"So am I, Son."

For most of the remainder of the trip back to the Ross place, they poled and paddled in uneventful silence. Before they left the run from Zeke's place, however, a large snake dropped into the boat from an overhanging limb. Sim automatically brought his pole across the reptile with a hard blow, then tossed it into the water.

Zeke said, "We sure have to watch out for them critters, don't we?"

"Yes, Sir, that we do," answered Sim. "We can't go to sleep on the job in this swamp."

The two men continued to glide through the swamp water, brown from the thick, acidic vegetation. The calming sounds, the canopies of overhanging limbs, and the unending beauty of the swamp were enough to lull the men into thoughts of the peace and tranquility all around them—in their homes, and among their friends. They felt no pity or envy toward the outlanders. Perhaps they possessed more worldly goods, and maybe they were able to travel to other parts of Georgia and to Florida. But Sim and Mr. Zeke believed that few people in the world knew the inner peace that their lives in the swamp land bestowed upon them and their families.

They were both thinking about the fish fry that Aggie had promised them upon their return. They would build a fire under the big black washpot filled with grease. Injun Joe had promised to supply enough fresh brim and perch for everyone, and Aggie and Fawn would prepare hushpuppies from cornmeal and seasoning, roll them into small balls, and drop them into the boiling grease along with the fish. There would be a big bowl of potato salad and plenty of hot coffee as well.

Mr. Zeke was roused from his thoughts when Sim stood up and made his holler. They were a good two miles from the Ross place, but Sim knew that everyone there could hear him. He was letting them know that they could start the fire and begin to get things ready.

As they neared the island, the aroma of fresh fish filled the soft warm air. Sim and Zeke looked forward to eating the fish and drinking some of Injun Joe's spirits—just enough to whet their appetites and help them overcome their fatigue from the trip.

When the two men climbed out of the small boat, they found that the delicious meal was ready. Joe and his family had even remained later than usual in order to take part in the frolic. Darkness would catch them away from home on this night, but that didn't bother Joe and his family. They all knew the way home, and these people were their friends.

By the time the meal was over and everything was cleaned up, the moon was high in the heavens and millions of stars peeped through the long-leafed pines that surrounded the Ross's island home. Mr. Jim threw some sulphur on the waning fire to ward off the mosquitoes, and everyone, including the Lightfoot family, gathered on the porch to pick and sing. Aggie had her banjo, Jim had his fiddle, and Zeke was tuning up his banjo. Without any prompting, Sim began to sing "The Turtle Dove," and his beautiful voice rang out in the vast expanse of trees and water. On the second verse, everyone joined in, and the fiddle and the two banjos picked up the tune and led the group into verse after verse of this lonesome song, a favorite of swamp people. Sim next led them in verses of "The Rabbit Song," "Daniel Spikes," and finally, with tears in his eyes, he slowly sang "Dixie." All were quiet as his beautiful voice echoed through the swamp land—even the birds and animals. After he sang the final words of the beloved song, everyone suddenly let forth a Rebel Yell, as if prompted by some unseen force. The yell may have sounded a little like the swamp holler, but Sim knew that they held the same pride he had felt so many times when his outfit gave the Rebel Yell before going into battle.

Finally, Mr. Jim called bedtime. The Lightfoot family left for home, and all the others were soon in their beds. Soon the only sounds to be heard were the screeching of a night owl and the distant splashing of animals as they sloshed among the water lilies and the cypresses in the surrounding water.

As the renovation neared completion, Aggie and Fawn finished the colorful curtains and hung them over the two small windows in the room. "Between the two of us," said Aggie, "we've done some right pretty sewin', Fawn. With the new dresses for you, Dawn, and me, and the shirts for the men, I think we've done a pretty good job."

"Everyone is very happy over the new clothes, Miss Aggie," said Fawn. "Joe strut like a big turkey when he try on his new shirt. We all will be at Mr. Sim's weddin'. He is a brave soldier, and deserves a nice, big weddin'."

"This is a happy time for all of us, Fawn. Some day your little ones will be gettin' married, and I hope you'll be as happy then as I am now."

When the time came for all the visitors to leave, they seemed reluctant to go. The wedding was fast approaching, however, and everyone needed to make the final preparations. Sim sent word to Min by Mr. Zeke that they would take two boats to the church so that Min would have room to bring any extra clothing or personal belongings that she needed for her new home.

Miss Ada and Min had done some beautiful sewing while the men were away. In better times, before the war had brought so much scarcity of goods, Ada had bought up white muslin and yards and yards of lace, hoping some day to make a wedding dress for her beautiful eldest daughter. She had spent hour after hour fitting the dress and sewing on the yards of lace. Ada had wanted such a dress for herself when she had married Zeke all those many years ago, but her family had been so poor that they were barely able to keep their children covered with the simplest of clothing. So now she was finally living the fantasy that she had had so long ago. Her daughter, with her curly blonde hair and beautiful complexion, would be the lovely bride that Ada had once dreamed of being. Ada knew that Min loved Sim, but no one could love more deeply than she herself loved Zeke. He had provided her with a good life and built a nice, comfortable house for her and their children. What more could anyone want from life?

Min had insisted that her mother and the younger girls each needed a new dress for the big occasion, and while Ada worked on the wedding dress, Min spent her time on the other dresses. She had learned well the art of dressmaking from her mother, and as a result, the other three dresses were very pretty, too.

By the time the Price men arrived home, Ada and Min had all the dresses pressed and hanging, just waiting for the big day. Min's other clothes and personal belongings were neatly packed and ready to go in the big carpet bag that the family possessed. Ada's mother had given it to Ada when she had married Zeke. There had been no need to use it since then, as Ada had not spent a night away from home in all these years. Of course she had kept the bag, especially since it was one of the few presents her family had been able to give her. Life had been hard for them, and they had barely been able to eke out a living for their family. They were good people, however, and Ada was proud of her family, no matter how poor they were. To her, there were so many things more important than an abundance of worldly possessions.

The wedding day dawned bright and beautiful. The birds sang happy tunes while the Price family dressed in their new clothes. The

Rosses as well as the Lightfoots dressed in their new finery, too, and all were soon on their way to the little church near Moniac.

When the families arrived, the church grounds were already filled with wagons and ox carts belonging to the outlanders who attended Bethel Church, and along the edge of the nearby run were the many boats of the island families. All of the church members were in a festive holiday mood and were dressed better than usual. Some were already setting up tables on the church grounds and piling them with plate after plate of good food.

The Ross, Price, and Lightfoot families met in a group and sat down at the front of the church. All others, except the women who were guarding the food, entered the church as well. The preacher thoughtfully gave a very short sermon and then asked Sim and Min to come to the alter.

Aggie and Ada could not hold back their tears as they watched their children go forward. How blessed they were to have Sim home from the war! How blessed they were that Min had been faithful to Sim and had waited patiently for his return! The couple stood alone before the minister as he performed the beautiful ceremony that made them husband and wife, and Aggie automatically took hold of Jim's big, rough hand. Ada reached for the work-worn hand of her beloved Zeke, and both couples wished only that their children would find the happiness that they themselves had known.

Finally, the minister announced to Sim that he could kiss the bride. A sigh of approval came from the congregation as the tall, dark groom kissed his pretty, golden-haired bride. The ceremony came to a joyful close, and everyone exited to the church grounds to offer their congratulations and best wishes for a long life of happiness together. The feast followed, and it was a happy day for the Bethel congregation.

The Lightfoot family were at first shyly hesitant to mingle with these people who were strangers to them. However, when Aggie introduced them to her friends as good neighbors to her family, the members of the congregation responded warmly and made them feel welcome.

Jake and Caleb were dispatched to their family's boats to load Min's possessions into Sim's boat. Min's younger sisters had made certain that there was plenty of rice available, and as the bride and groom walked arm-in-arm toward the boats, there were showers and showers of rice, and well wishes from all. The remainder of those present lingered for a while, reluctant to break up such a happy gathering.

Sim lifted his bride into the boat and slowly poled their way down the run to open water. Before he lifted the paddle to row them across the big lake, he took Min in his arms and assured her that he was the happiest man in the world.

"Oh, Sim," Min responded, "I am so happy, and we'll always be happy together, forever and ever."

"I know we will be, Min. I just know we will be."

They reached the Ross place well before Jim and Aggie. When Sim unloaded the boat and led her in to see their new room, Min told him that she had never seen a room so beautiful. The curtains, the furniture, and the pretty mirror were luxuries beyond anything she had ever seen.

"These ain't all the nice things I'll have for you some day, Honey," promised Sim. "Just you wait and see."

"I won't ever need anything else that I don't have right now."

After a moment, they heard the sound of the other boat approaching, followed by Jim's swamp holler. They both ran out to greet Jim and Aggie.

"Welcome to your new home, Min," they both said in unison.

"Our room is the most beautiful place in the world, and I do thank you for everything," said Min, as she hugged both of Sim's parents.

"All we ask is for both of you to be happy," said Aggie.

"Aggie's right, children. You both just make yourselves at home now," added Jim.

"Thanks for everything, Pa," said Sim. "All we want is to be as happy as you two have always been."

"You will, Son," replied Jim. "I know you will."

As they stood smiling at each other, Min knew that she did indeed belong in the Ross household, and that she would always feel welcome there.

The days following Sim and Min's wedding were filled with happiness. There was little work to be done on the farm at that time of year, so the two young people took short trips to the nearby towns so that Min could become more familiar with her new surroundings. They poled their way around the south swamp, drove the ox cart to Traders Hill, and visited the settlement at St. George.

Min was fascinated by Traders Hill. She had never been to a town of any size before. She had visited the little settlement of Fargo down the river from the Price home, but other than that, she had spent most of her life close to the Price home. She was amazed by the beautiful St. Marys River, and Sim promised her that one day he would take her to the town of St. Marys and maybe as far as Jacksonville, down in Florida.

Min loved Sim's beautiful horse, Bob, and Sim taught her to ride him. Soon she was spending hours riding around the island, careful not to stray out of hollering distance. Although she was not afraid of the swamp, she knew that there were certain dangers that she might encounter. Snakes and wild animals were certainly hazards to avoid, but young women living around the swamp had to look out for dangerous people, as well. Many outlanders had recently come into the area to hunt and fish, and there were still a few young men living in the swamp to evade the Confederate draft. One man in particular seemed a bit eccentric, but the Ross family thought that he was actually harmless. They called him "Crazy Harry," but Mr. Jim thought that Harry just pretended to be insane in order to keep from being drafted. Whatever the explanation, his very appearance could frighten anyone who didn't know him. The only real harm he seemed to inflict on people was stealing their chickens and the vegetables from their gardens. He would ease in during the night, get his supply of food, and be gone before anyone could get a shotgun and go after him. If there were dogs in the yards, Crazy Harry had some way of charming them into silence while he secured his supplies. The men were not afraid of Harry, but Sim warned Min that it might be a different story altogether if Harry spotted a pretty young woman out alone.

One day during this time the young couple visited the Lightfoot family. Joe showed Min the family's stills and sent them home loaded with spirits for Mr. Jim and a good supply of fresh fish for supper. Little Dawn and Pete were charmed by Mr. Sim's golden-haired wife, and Min and Sim invited them to come over soon for a cookout and singing.

At the Ross home, whenever Miss Aggie went about her household chores, Min insisted that Aggie allow her to help. Min's life at home had consisted of a lot of hard work, and she quickly proved to be a great help with the cooking and other household chores. A closeness developed between the two women, and Aggie felt that she finally had the daughter she had always wanted. While the men hunted and worked in the fields, Aggie and Min decided to make some dresses for themselves and some shirts for Mr. Jim and Sim. They still had several bolts of the cloth that Jim had bought from the Yankee merchant, so Min was able to show Aggie her ability as a seamstress. Aggie could sew nice garments, but Min's quick young hands were amazing to watch as she expertly transformed the material into pretty dresses.

One afternoon while they were deeply involved in the dressmaking, Min had a request to make of Aggie. "Miss Aggie," she began, "I know you and Mr. Jim learned to read and write when you lived in the Carolinas, and you taught Sim to read and write, too. Well, my Pa and Ma had almost no schooling, 'cause they lived in the piny woods over in Florida. They can sign their names and do a little readin'. They taught us children that much, but I want to know how to read and write so Sim will be proud of me. I can't even read the words in the little song book at church."

"I thank you for askin' me, honey," responded Aggie. "I'll be glad to teach you, just like I did Sim when he was a little boy. It'll likely take a while, but we'll get on it right away."

"I know I could've asked Sim to teach me, but somehow I just feel a little shy about askin' him to teach me what I should've learned as a child."

"I understand, Min. I would feel the same way. This'll be our own project."

As the weeks passed, Aggie and Min secretly worked on their "project" together. Aggie found that Min learned very fast, and the two women both enjoyed the lessons. Min assured her mother-in-law that when she had children, she would teach them to read and write, too.

Early one morning, Mr. Zeke sent Jake and Caleb over to the Ross's place to invite everyone to a party the following day. The Prices had not seen Min since the wedding, and they missed her very much. Everyone had such a good time that the Rosses soon hosted a similar party of their own. The crops on both islands had to be worked, but these happy occasions were worth a little extra work another day.

Aggie had her own vegetable garden, and Min insisted upon doing her part of the work there, too. As in other chores, the two women worked happily together. They cultivated tomatoes, beans, peas, sweet potatoes, Irish potatoes, and corn. Meanwhile, the men tended the sugar cane and the small patches of cotton. With Sim's young, able-bodied help, Jim saw fit to clear more land of the pines that grew in abundance on the island. Some day he hoped to sell timber, but for now he just needed to clear the land to make room for more crops, and he could use the timber for firewood.

Every day more men from the outside came in to hunt for alligators and the furry animals which were abundant in the swamp. The Ross family did not resent this infringement by the outlanders. In fact, there was such an overabundance of wild animals that the Ross men had been forced to build fences around their gardens and fields to keep out the deer, bears, rabbits, and boars that wreaked havoc on their crops and occasionally proved dangerous to people.

The Ross family had begun to make friends with many of the new outsiders who came into the swamp to hunt and fish. Some were simply hunting alligators. In fact, the new market for alligator hides was developing so well that Sim joined the hunters in making a profit from these hides.

The Ross family was especially glad to see the hunters weed out some of the bears. These animals had killed many of their pigs over the years, and pork, along with deer, was their chief source of meat. There were plenty of chickens, but even they were occasionally killed by wild animals.

As more and more hunters came into the swamp, they soon found that the Ross home was a good place to stop for cool water and a visit. If Sim and Mr. Jim were not too busy on the homeplace, they would sometimes accompany the outlanders and help them with their hunt, and the visitors in turn kept the Ross family in touch with the outside world. The hunters often brought newspapers so that the Rosses could learn what was happening to the South following the end of the war. Sim's blood almost boiled when he read about the continuous punishment of the southern states and about the poverty that was gripping the South. But he knew that there was no longer anything he could do about that. After all, the war was over. All Sim could do now was help take care of his family and be grateful that they were so far removed from the things that were happening outside the swamp.

Both of Sim and Min's families looked forward to the monthly sermons at Bethel Church. Not only did it give them a good chance to visit each other, but they could visit with their other friends as well. Sim and Min particularly enjoyed the visits to church, because they were now leading the singing. Since most of the swampers did not read well, Sim and Min could help them learn the words and tunes.

During the first year Sim was home from the war, not only had he taken a leadership position in his church, but he had also married the most beautiful woman in the swamp. He had helped improve the homeplace, made quite a bit of money from the sale of hides to the outlanders, and used most of the money to buy small parcels of land that became available from state grants. Many of the Indians were already leaving for the Florida Everglades, and as they left, their land became available for purchase. The Ross family was very grateful that Joe and his family still seemed content to remain in the Georgia swamps. They knew they would miss the Lightfoot family if they decided to follow their kinsmen and friends to south Florida.

The greatest joy for Sim during his first year home, however, was Min's announcement that she was expecting a child. Both families were very excited, and Miss Aggie and Min went to work immediately on baby clothes and new expandable dresses for Min. Every plan that involved the Ross family seemed to revolve around the time when Min's baby was due. Aggie was not experienced in assisting during a birth, but Fawn was a trusted midwife who was fully alerted to the situation. Aggie would do what she could, but she would put her full trust in Fawn. Whatever herbs and Indian medicine that Fawn used must have been good, because the word among the swamp people was that her methods worked.

At last, the day came when Min knew that the baby was on the way. Everyone was excited, but Aggie cautioned the men to be as calm as possible. Mr. Jim left to fetch Fawn, and Sim stayed at the bedside of his wife. Aggie got all of the needed supplies ready for Min and her baby. Although Min insisted that she was fine, Aggie was not convinced, and she was very relieved when Fawn arrived and took charge.

The family tried to go about their daily routines, but as the hours wore on and on, Aggie was beginning to get very worried. She attempted to hide her fears from Sim, who had not budged from Min's bedside. Meanwhile, Jim was pacing up and down the porch as though his own wife were the one having a baby.

After several hours, Sim emerged from Min's room and sought consolation from his mother. Tears ran down his face as he asked, "Is there something wrong, Ma? Does it usually take this long?"

"Oh, I don't think there's anything wrong, Son," answered Aggie. "Some women just take longer than others. You just stay out here with your Pa, and I'll go in and sit with Fawn and Min."

Aggie entered the room, and when she saw Min's exhausted face, she grew even more worried. "Do you think she'll soon deliver this baby, Fawn?" she asked.

"She's tryin', Miss Aggie, but that's a stubborn baby. It'll come after 'while," answered Fawn.

She began to administer potions from the bag she had brought with her, all the while quietly chanting in her Indian tongue. She placed her hand on Min's wet forehead and chanted a little louder. Aggie did not know what to make of the ordeal; she had never seen Fawn ply her skills before. Aggie moved to the other side of the bed to let Min know that she was not alone and to offer her some measure of comfort.

"Now, Miss Min, try very hard and do your part—very hard, and the baby will come," Fawn ordered.

Min did as she was told, and suddenly Fawn and Aggie were very busy attending to a screaming baby girl. Fawn told Aggie to take the baby while she saw to Min's needs, and both women were so busy that they did not see Sim and Mr. Jim ease open the door and ask if everything was all right.

"Almost ready, Mr. Sim," answered Fawn. "In a minute, you can come see your beautiful baby girl with golden hair like her mother's. She took a long time, but everything's all right now. Miss Min may not have any more babies; she's had a hard time, but this one's fine."

What she said did not register on Sim. He was too busy rushing to his wife's side.

Min smiled at him then. "We have a beautiful daughter, Sim. She even has a little crown of golden hair. What will we name her?"

"Let's name her Queen, 'cause some day she's gonna be the queen of this swamp. Will that suit you, Min?"

"That's fine, Sim, just fine," she answered. She was really too tired to worry about names or queens or anything else at that point. She was dropping off to sleep when Aggie carefully handed the baby to Sim. When the tiny infant opened her bright blue eyes, Sim knew that he was hooked for life.

"She's my little bundle of gold," said Sim. "No real gold could ever be as precious."

He gently passed the baby back to Aggie, who tucked her in beside her mother. Min was already fast asleep, but Sim remained by his wife and baby while Aggie and Fawn retreated to the kitchen for some coffee and much-needed rest. Mr. Jim eased into the room to sit with his son for a while and to feast his eyes on his beautiful grandchild.

When the two women were finally seated in the kitchen, Aggie asked Fawn what she had meant about Min not having another child.

"Miss Min had a very hard time," answered Fawn. "I'm afraid that some damage has been done, but maybe not. We'll just have to wait and see."

Aggie did not want to believe this, so for the present she put it out of her mind. She asked that Fawn remain for a while, until they were sure that Min and the baby were really all right.

In the meantime, Jim prepared to leave for the Price home. He planned to deliver the good news to Min's family and hopefully bring Miss Ada back with him so that she could be with Min and the baby for the first few days after the ordeal of childbirth. Aggie was anxious for Ada to come. This was a new experience for her. She had had her only baby twenty-two years ago, and Ada had had much more experience with childbearing. And after all, this was her own daughter who had just gone through several critical hours in order to bring her baby into the world, and Aggie knew that Ada would want to see her.

Chapter Four

☾

After Ada had spent a week with her daughter and the rest of the Ross family, she decided that she should return home to look after her own family. Just as she was packing her clothes and getting ready for Jim to take her across the swamp, they heard a familiar holler.

"That must be Zeke," said Ada. "I knew he couldn't wait much longer to see his grandbaby!"

As Zeke docked his boat, Ada met him with the good news that Min and the baby were both fine. "Come and see the prettiest baby in the world, Zeke," she said. "She's even prettier than her Ma was when she was born."

After several hours of visiting and playing with the baby, Zeke had to agree with his wife. Seeing that Aggie was ready to go home, he was glad he could save Jim the trip across the swamp. He was reluctant to leave his grandchild, even after several hours' visit, so they promised to return soon.

Min was soon out of bed and able to attend to her child, but Aggie curtailed her housework, even when she grew stronger. Min enjoyed sitting on the front porch and rocking little Queenie, as they were now calling the baby. Min sang to her as they rocked and the cool, damp breezes ruffled the leaves of the Chinaberry trees in the front yard.

On one such occasion, Min noticed a small boat docking down at the landing, and a very ragged man came ashore without the usual swamp holler. He had a long beard, and his appearance was quite frightening. Luckily, Aggie was sitting on the porch with Min and the baby, and when Min expressed her concern, Aggie told her not to worry. "That's Crazy Harry," she said. "He don't mean no harm. I'll go down and meet him at the gate."

Aggie would have felt a little more comfortable if Jim or Sim had been close by, but they were off on an alligator hunt. Before she left the house to walk down to the gate, she quietly reminded Min of the location of the shotgun, adding that she felt sure it would not be needed.

Aggie greeted Harry as though he were a good friend and asked what she could do for him.

"Evenin', Ma'am," said Harry. "Just want to give little wagon to golden-haired baby. I make it myself."

"Oh, thank you, Harry," said Aggie. "Do come by and see the baby. She will be so proud of her new wagon."

Harry removed his floppy hat and followed Aggie to the edge of the porch. Aggie introduced her daughter-in-law, and Harry handed the little wagon to Aggie when Min held the baby up so that he could get a good look at her. They invited Harry to come in and sit a spell, but he just stood in the yard looking very uncomfortable.

"Very pretty golden-haired baby, Miz Ross. I make more toys for golden baby. I love children, 'specially Ross baby."

"We thank you, Mr. Harry," said Min. "You are very kind. I'll take good care of the little wagon until Queenie is old enough to ride in it."

"Thankee, Ma'am. Queenie Ross—pretty name, pretty child," muttered Harry as he turned toward the gate and his boat.

"How on earth did he know about the baby, Miss Aggie?" asked Min once Harry was out of earshot.

"I sometimes think that Harry knows everythin' that goes on in this swamp. Many times you can see him lurkin' in the woods near the barn out there. If Jim walks toward him, he'll usually disappear in a hurry. We see him most often when we're a singin' on the front porch. Jim called to him to come and join us one night, but he just scampered away. Since then, when we see him out there, we don't say nothin', just let him stay there in the woods and maybe feel like he's a part of us."

The little wagon was only the first of many toys that Harry made for Queenie. He usually brought them by when no one was around to see him. Occasionally some member of the family would spot him late at night or very early in the morning leaving a toy on the top of a fence post. Sometimes it was a doll made from corn shucks, sometimes it was an animal carved from wood. Once there was even a small pig tied to the gate. The Rosses wished that Harry would come by with his gifts during the day so they could thank him, but that was not Harry's way. But everyone still felt that Crazy Harry was keeping careful watch on the progress of the Ross baby.

After Queenie was born, Harry no longer stole the Ross's chickens or any vegetables from their garden. It was as if he were showing respect for the little baby and her family. Since all of the toys were left without any chance for the Ross family to thank Harry, they decided to repay his kindness by leaving presents for him by the front gate. Sometimes it was a watermelon or a few cantaloupes; at times they would leave a basket of peas, beans, corn, or some other food that wouldn't spoil if Harry didn't come by for a day or so. Eventually their gifts would disappear. Harry didn't always leave a toy, but when he did, it was always a work of art. The wood carvings of swamp animals were especially beautiful. Queenie was soon old enough to play with them, and Min used them to teach her the names of the animals.

The Ross family had settled back to its regular routine. Queenie was growing up quickly; before the family realized it, she was beginning to crawl around on her pallet and was soon trying to form words. Sim sat for hours and just watched his little girl, all the while making plans for her to join him out in the swamp when she was old enough to hunt and fish with him.

"Sim, you are gonna spoil that child," scolded Min as she watched her husband play with the baby and tell her all the nice things she would have one day.

"Oh, that's all right, Honey. I can't help spoiling this little lump of gold," said Sim. "Besides, I think her Ma and her Grandma and Grandpa are just as guilty of the same thing."

"It won't hurt her," interjected Aggie. "Jim and me, we spoiled Sim, and look how fine he turned out."

"I can't argue against that, Miss Aggie," laughed Min.

Mr. Jim sat close by, grinning from ear to ear because he knew that he was the worst spoiler of all. He talked to Queenie and played with her for hours at a time, and he was clearly a favorite of her playmates. "Well, one thing for sure, I don't spoil her none," he said. The others laughed.

Dawn and Pete came over to play with Queenie whenever they could talk their parents into taking them to the Ross place. Even though they were older than Queenie, they still enjoyed playing with her. She responded to their attention and laughed enthusiastically at their antics. Dawn encouraged the baby to talk and even tried to teach her a few Indian words.

Miss Aggie and Min delighted in making pretty clothes for Queenie. Their friends at church looked forward to seeing the Ross baby and the pretty dresses she wore on preaching Sundays. Min's family was also happy to see little Queenie at church, and as frequently as possible at the Ross place. Very often the Rosses would hear an unexpected holler whenever a member of the Price family paid a surprise visit.

Sim's alligator hides were bringing in a good bit of cash. On one trip when he was taking these hides to Traders Hill, Sim finally felt free to buy the gold ring he had always wanted for Min. He found a gold band at a little store that sold jewelry, and a man who worked there engraved an "M" and an "S" inside the ring. Min was delighted with the ring and hoped some day to pass it on to Queenie.

With Jim's help, Sim added a small room for Queenie onto their room. She loved to show it to her playmates, and by the time she was walking, she was following the Lightfoot children all around the yard, into the woods, and on rides in the boats. They taught her the ways of the swamps and pointed out the dangerous plants and animals.

By 1870, the outlanders were beginning to buy up timbered land for the sawmills. The railroads were creeping up from Florida and across the swamp lands in South Georgia as well. Railroads required cypress logs for crossties, and the demand for the wood was growing steadily. Sim talked the situation over with Jim, and both men decided that the time had come for them to buy more timbered land. They wanted to try to get the Confederate gold off their hands and use it to buy the Indian land that was becoming available as well as some of the local land that the State of Georgia was releasing for sale.

Sim had been planning this for some time. A very nice young banker from St. Marys had recently been making more and more hunting trips into the swamp. This young man, Henry Cooper, admired Sim because of his war record. Henry had wanted very much to fight for the South, but he had been born crippled, so there was no way he could serve in the army. He had managed to make quite a bit of money during the war and had opened a bank at St. Marys. Under Henry's careful direction, the bank had continued to prosper even during Reconstruction.

A deep friendship developed between the two young men, and they often hunted and fished together. There were other places where Henry could have gone for recreation, but he always chose the south swamp. Even when Sim was busy on a hunt elsewhere in the swamp, Henry always went by the Ross place for a visit, and he always had a gift for Queenie. Henry was married but had no children of his own, so he delighted in lavishing toys and other gifts on the golden-haired baby in his favorite area of the swamp.

Sim learned from Henry that most of the Yankee soldiers had moved out of southeast Georgia. In fact, most people who were originally from the North had moved away altogether. The area itself was now very poor, so there was little to keep an outsider there.

As the friendship between Sim and Henry grew, Sim began to wonder if Henry could handle his Confederate gold and maybe help him purchase some land. He talked this idea over with Jim, who agreed. Sim still made no mention of his treasure to Min. Men usually attended to such business matters, so there was no reason for him to worry his wife. When he finally had the matter settled, he would then explain it all to her. But first he had to decide if he could risk his secret with his friend. As honest and upright as Henry Cooper seemed, Sim wondered if he could be trusted with something this serious. Sim thought Henry could be trusted, but he decided to think on it a while longer.

Sim did think about his plan for several weeks, and in the meantime he talked at length with his parents about his decision. Both Jim and Aggie felt that Henry was trustworthy and would advise Sim on how to proceed with his plans for putting the gold into circulation. Henry had connections with the Jacksonville banks and with the state people who handled the land sales, so he seemed the ideal person to take charge of their plans for the land acquisition and for the handling of the Confederate gold.

Several weeks passed before Henry Cooper returned to the swamp for a fishing trip, and Sim made a point of going with him. He felt that it would be a good time to confide in his friend and get his advice on the disposal of the gold.

Without knowing it, Henry gave Sim an easy opening for the conversation. "You know, Sim," Henry said, "lots of this swamp land is coming on the market now. If you have any ready money, it might be wise for you to buy up as much of the south swamp as you can."

"I've been thinkin' on this, too," responded Sim. "I do have a little money saved, but I'm afraid that wouldn't buy much land. I do, however, have somethin' stashed away that I believe would be of a little value."

He then swore Henry to secrecy. They shook hands as Henry assured his friend that his word was his bond. Henry was anxious to know what his friend had in mind that was such a secret, but he was a patient man and waited for Sim to proceed. Sim started at the beginning, describing the escape from Richmond and his fast ride through Georgia after President Davis's capture. He explained how the gold had been thrust upon him without his knowledge and described his fear that he would be hunted down by the Federal soldiers. He told Henry that the gold was buried in a safe place but that he had always planned to trade it in for land some day. "I want you to know that I am honest, and that all I have told you is true. I just hope you can help me get it off my hands without gettin' into any trouble," he concluded.

"I don't doubt for a minute that you are honest, Sim," Henry said. "You certainly did the right thing. If you had turned it over to the Federal troops in this district, I doubt it would have ever reached the government in Washington. The Federals looted and stole so much all over the South, especially in Georgia. They took everything—jewelry, china, silverware, money, livestock, whatever they could find. I'd rather have seen that gold dropped into the Atlantic Ocean than have it fall into the hands of those ravaging Yankees."

"That's how I felt, and my parents encouraged me to hide it for a while. So that's what I did. What do you think I should do now?"

"I think I can take care of it, Sim, but let's leave it where it is for now. In the meantime, I'll make contact with a close banker friend in Jacksonville. He's a full-blooded southerner, and he was in the Confederate army. He can be trusted. If he thinks that it's not safe to bring it out right now, he'll tell us. I do have access to the land that's coming up for sale, so I can help you there. I think it would be best to buy a small amount of land at first. You don't want to draw too much attention to your having access to a good deal of money all at one time. Then we can keep most of your money on deposit in Jacksonville and bring just a small amount to my bank at St. Marys. Do you have any idea of the value of your gold, Sim?"

"None at all. I'm curious 'bout that too, but I actually have no way of knowin' its value."

"Well, don't worry about it. I'll look into the situation and let you know what I learn as soon as I can."

Sim had no doubt that Henry would keep his secret. They finished their fishing trip on a pleasant note, and Henry returned to his home in St. Marys.

While Min was putting Queenie to bed that night, Sim took his parents aside and told them the encouraging news. Jim and Aggie felt quite relieved because they believed that Henry could be trusted. Sim hadn't told Henry where the gold was buried, and Henry had not asked. Maybe, just maybe, Sim would soon own so much of the swamp land that in the years to come, little Queenie would indeed be queen of the swamp!

Sim was very anxious to tell Min about the gold and about his plans, but he decided to wait until Henry investigated the matter. That way she wouldn't be disappointed if the plans did not materialize. He fell asleep that night thinking of all the nice things he could give his wife and child, as well as his parents, if Henry's plan worked out.

After three weeks, they heard a familiar holler. Sim had taught Henry Cooper how to make the swamp holler, but, as with most outlanders, it was not quite perfected. Nevertheless, it was a welcome sound, and little four-year-old Queenie ran down to the boat landing to welcome him. Dawn and Pete were playing with Queenie, and they ran down to welcome the visitor, too. Luckily, Henry had brought several little picture books for Queenie, and when he saw her Indian playmates, he divided the gifts among the three children.

In the meantime, Sim had gone down to the landing to greet his friend. When the children scampered up to the yard to play, Sim and Henry remained at the landing to talk business. Henry had had good luck with his banker friend in Jacksonville. The banker was anxious to know how much gold was there, but Henry of course had no idea of the amount involved.

"We had no idea how to judge its worth, but it was heavy. It almost weighed my horse down," said Sim.

"If you'll trust me with the evaluation, I'll meet you a week from today at Traders Hill. Since I'll be alone, I'll arm myself. Some right rough characters live down this way, as you well know. I would advise you to bring Mr. Jim along, and both of you should carry a gun." The two men decided on the exact time and place to meet at Traders Hill, then walked up to the house. Henry did not have time for a fishing trip, but he did want to stay for a short visit with the Ross family. Soon he was on his way back to the landing on the edge of the swamp where he had left his horse.

Mr. Jim was anxious to know what Henry had had to say. He asked Sim to go with him to check on some vegetables he had planted, so Sim was able to relate Henry's conversation to his Pa in private.

"It sounds good, Son. Henry's a very careful man. I think his advice about taking the guns along is a good idea."

"I guess now's the time for me to tell Min. I don't want to get her hopes up, though, so I'll try to be careful what I say, and I'll ask her not to tell anybody else about it. It likely won't be worth much, anyway."

"Well, we'll wait 'til after dark to do our diggin'," said Jim. "We'll have to make sure that Crazy Harry ain't out there checkin' on us."

"I had the same thought, Pa. I think it'd also be best to wait 'til the night before we plan to take our package to Traders Hill."

Jim agreed, and as the men were walking back toward the house, Sim was thinking of the best way to break the news to Min. He wanted to play down the whole story. He didn't want her to get excited over the gold and then be disappointed if they found out that it wasn't worth very much. As far as Sim knew, it might not be of much value, but it would still be a relief to get it off his hands. He did not want to go on for the rest of his life thinking that someone from the federal government might come looking for him and maybe put him in jail for having part of the treasure that the federal government thought should have been turned over to them.

The war had been over for five years, but Reconstruction had not ended. The newspapers that Henry shared with Sim described the suffering in Atlanta and in other states. The South was trying to rebuild, but in those lean years, they had very little with which to rebuild. Their Confederate money was worthless, and there was almost no labor left on the farms. The slaves had been freed, but most of them were left without any means to make a living. Sim had never believed in slavery, and he was grateful that he had been born and reared in a part of Georgia where slaves were not used for labor. His people worked their own land and provided a living for their families. They did not believe that one person could own another. Sim knew that some people who owned plantations over on the coast had owned slaves, but they were gone now. From what he could learn, some of the former slaves in southeast Georgia who had not gone north were working on the farms for wages or as sharecroppers. Most of them, however, were working for the sawmills that were springing up. Sim was glad that some of the black folks could find work, and he was grateful that the swamp people were not among the Georgians who had owned these former slaves.

That evening, Sim made time to tell Min his story. He first swore her to secrecy, then he made her promise not to tell Queenie. He would tell his daughter this story some day, but not now. He could easily imagine her telling Dawn and Pete the whole story, and that could prove very dangerous. Then, while Min listened patiently without interrupting, he told her the entire story.

"I still don't want you to get your hopes up, Min, 'cause this whole thing may not work out," he cautioned.

Min had remained very calm through the whole story, and she now responded very sensibly. "You're right about not gettin' excited, Sim. You did right to hide it. The only thing that worries me is that if the gold does prove to be valuable, I'm afraid you might want to move out of the swamp."

"Oh, no," Sim assured her. Then he chuckled. "I was afraid that you might want to move out. There's no other place on earth I'd rather live. But if you ever want to move out, I'll try to please you. Of course, we've got to think of what's best for Queenie, too, but I'm thinkin' she'll love the swamp like I do. Anyway, I'm hopin' to buy land with the money I get, but we'll have more spendin' money, too. The main thing now is not to get our hopes up too high so we won't be disappointed if it don't work out. I don't know what that gold's worth, and Henry ain't seen it yet, so it may just be a wild goose chase. Anyway, it'll likely be a while before Henry can get this settled. Remember, too, there's always the chance that things could go all wrong, and I could be accused of stealing from the government. I would have no way to prove I'm innocent, because I don't know where any of my cavalry buddies are, and I have no way to find out. So you see that I'm actually takin' a big chance in all this. That's why I'm askin' you not to mention it to a soul."

At sundown, on the day before they were to meet Henry at Traders Hill, Sim and Mr. Jim scouted the woods around the house to be sure they were not observed by Crazy Harry or anyone else. Queenie had been put to bed, and Aggie and Min were keeping watch on the front porch in case someone should come up the run and stop down at the boat landing. When they knew that it was safe, Jim and Sim went quietly to the back yard, dug the metal box from the ground, and replanted the bush that had grown over it for so many years. Sim put the box in a crocus sack and carried it to his parents' room in the house.

The two women had closed all the shutters and turned the lamps down very low. Aggie felt safer with Jim's pistol on a table by one of the lamps. Min checked to see that Queenie was sound asleep, then returned to the bedroom with Aggie. They all closed the door behind them, and Sim lifted the box from the sack and began to open it. It had been closed and bolted so firmly that he had to exert quite a bit of effort to open it. When Sim finally removed the lid, Min saw a sight that she had never imagined possible. She started to let out a screech but clamped her hand over her mouth. "Heaven help us, Sim," she whispered. "I ain't never seen nothin' like this!"

There it was: pure, shiny yellow gold—not a great amount, but enough. It had to be valuable, but Min, like the others, had no idea how much it was worth.

"It's excitin', ain't it, Min?" breathed Aggie. She remembered the excitement she had felt the first night Sim was home from the war and had shown it to them. How long ago that seemed! So many good things had already happened since then, and Aggie hoped that the gold would now only change their lives for the better. She knew that Jim wanted their son to buy land with any money they could get, whether it was from alligator hides or the sale of trees on the land they already owned. If they kept purchasing land, Jim expected that they would some day own most of the south swamp. The only worry Aggie had now was whether or not Sim would get into trouble when he turned the treasure over to the bankers. She hoped and prayed that he would not. The last five years had been such happy ones. She did not want the money to adversely affect any of their lives.

The following morning Sim and his Pa were up early loading the ox cart. Aggie and Min had packed a good lunch for them, and this was loaded into the cart along with the gold. The two men hoped to be back before dark but cautioned the women not to worry if they were late. Even though they wouldn't admit it, both men were apprehensive. Anything could go wrong. The cart could break down; Henry could be sick or get delayed. There was no way to communicate with him except to meet him as planned. If Henry was unable to meet them, they would simply return home with the "cargo" and wait for Henry to contact them.

Aggie made a list of some supplies they needed from Traders Hill and made sure that Jim had enough of her chicken and egg money to cover the cost of their purchases. "If you're able to give the gold to Henry, then maybe you could go do some shopping," she said. "I think there's enough money there to get Queenie a little toy, too." She sighed. "I keep thinkin' of all the things that could go wrong, but I hope they won't."

"Now, don't go gettin' anxious, Aggie," said Jim. "We'll be real careful, and if Henry's alive and well, he'll be there, I'm sure of it."

Sim peeked in at his sleeping daughter, told his wife and Ma goodbye, and he and Jim climbed onto the little ox cart. Sim had made many trips to Traders Hill over the last five years, and each time he had worn old clothes and the slouch hat that covered most of his face. Even on this day both Jim and he were dressed as though they were going hunting or fishing. Sim hated to transact business looking so pathetic, but Henry would understand. Somehow he thought that Henry might be in his swamp-fishing clothes, too. Maybe in years to come, if things worked out well, they could make trips to the bank at St. Marys dressed like the outlanders. But that was looking too far ahead. For now, the guns were in place, the gold was secure in the cart, and before the sun peeped through the trees, they headed toward Traders Hill and whatever awaited them there.

Chapter Five

☾

Sim and his father were deep in thought as they rode along in the early morning light. The beauty around them was breathtaking. A light breeze stirred the low-hanging moss and the branches of the trees. Squirrels scampered from limb to limb, and birds sang early morning greetings as they flitted from tree to tree.

"Pa, why would anybody ever want to live anywhere else but here?" asked Sim.

"I don't rightly know, Son. Of course, it just happened that me and your Ma settled here. It was just some place to settle away from Carolina, but mainly it was because the state was offerin' land to settlers. Lots of Indians were movin' out, and we had nothin', I mean nothin'. I look back now and wonder how we had the nerve to run away from our folks like that. But there was no way I could leave Aggie to marry that old man. Her life would have been hell on earth."

"You did right, Pa. I know Ma has always been happy here, even though she probably misses her folks sometimes. But if this package we're carryin' works out, I hope we can do somethin' real nice for Ma."

"Maybe it will make life a little easier for all of us," Jim added.

After this exchange, they rode along in silence. The going was quite rough, but their ox pulled the little cart steadily along toward the river. When they reached the river, the going was much easier, and they moved toward Traders Hill at a good pace.

The location where they were to meet Henry was a spot at the edge of town where visitors parked their wagons and buggies and hitched their horses. When they first saw Henry, they did not recognize him. He was dressed like a typical country man who had just come to town to do some trading. When he came over to greet them, he suggested that they follow him to a small farm he owned about a mile out of town. He hoped some day to have a tenant farmer live there and develop it into a profitable working farm. But for now, the house provided a place for him to spend the night when he had to conduct business in Traders Hill.

Sim drove the ox cart behind Henry's buggy until they reached the farm house. The two Ross men complemented the house and told Henry he was fortunate to have it. Compared to their home in the swamp, it was a place of considerable luxury.

"Now, I'm going to give you a key to this place, and I want you to feel free to use it any time you come over to Traders Hill," said Henry. "It'll also give us a place to meet when we have business to transact. You can spend the night here and not have to rush back home the same day.

"When I bought this place, my brother was against the war. He didn't want to be drafted, so I let him hide out here. I knew that he would never have been drafted, because he's slightly retarded. But I could never convince him that the Confederates wouldn't bother him. So instead of moving up here, he joined a group of young men who were heading out west. I haven't heard from him since. I hope he's all right, but I guess I'll never know.

"Anyway, let's get down to business. Is the gold in that box?"

"This is it, Henry," answered Sim, as he pried it open.

"Good lord!" exclaimed Henry, when he saw the gold. He couldn't resist the urge to touch the gleaming contents of the box.

"Well, I believe you have a handsome treasure here, and I really don't think you'll have anything to worry about. I keep hearing rumors of small amounts of Confederate money showing up here and there. My banker friend in Jacksonville even had some of the coins dribble into his bank. One rumor I've heard is that a very prominent Confederate leader was hoping to escape to England to avoid capture by the Federals, but he was destitute. So in order to help him, some Confederate troops took a sack of gold coins and threw it over his fence. I guess he received it, because apparently he did get to England. Frankly, from what I hear, I doubt that anyone who came into possession of any Confederate gold sent it on to Washington."

Sim was relieved at Henry's reassuring remarks. The men shared the lunch that Min and Aggie had packed, then they loaded the gold into Henry's buggy. Henry gave them a key to the house and insisted once more that they stay there whenever they wanted. After making plans to meet there again in one month, Henry left for his home in St. Marys. He would be late getting home, but if dark caught him, he had friends along the way with whom he could spend the night. He hoped this would not be necessary, however, because he was anxious to get the money to the safe in his bank.

Sim and his father left the house and went shopping feeling much more at ease. The gold was finally off their hands! Maybe it wouldn't amount to much, but at least they had lifted a burden by turning it over to Henry, whom they trusted completely.

"Well, Pa," said Sim, "we don't have much money for shopping today, but we don't need much, do we? At least we can get what Ma needs for the house, then maybe we'll buy some kind of surprise for our three women."

"That's a good idea, Son. I do think, though, that Henry was pleased with the contents of that box. I'm thinkin' things are gonna work out fine for all of us."

It was late when they reached home that night. Queenie had tried to wait up for them but had not been able to stay awake. Sim tiptoed into her little room and placed the small doll he had bought for her on the bed beside her. He kissed his sleeping daughter and whispered to her, "Baby, I do believe you really will be queen of this swamp one day."

Aggie and Min were pleased with the outcome of the trip. They all agreed to one thing—if they did come out well with the money, they would be very careful never to make a show of what they had. Their life in the south swamp was the only life they wanted. They didn't want to show off before the other swamp families. Their neighbors were too important to them, and if they made a big thing of having more worldly goods than those around them, they would drive their friends away. Nevertheless, they all went to bed that night thinking that all was well in their world and wondering how much of the south swamp would eventually belong to them.

During the next month, they busied themselves with their regular chores. The sugar cane crop had turned out quite well, and they made plans to have a big cane grinding. They had built a small sugar house behind the main house with a large vat for boiling the cane juice, which was pressed out of the cane in an ox-driven mill in the back yard. This juice would be boiled down to make syrup—or "lassies," as they called it—as well as the heavy brown sugar. Much of this sugar would then go into the stills to make spirits, and some of the juice would be used to make cane buck. Everyone at the cane grinding always looked forward to the buck, a favorite alcoholic drink which was made from fermented cane juice.

Bob could have easily been hitched to the mill, but Queenie had claimed him for her personal horse and would not hear of his being put to such menial labor. She could now ride Bob without being attended by an adult, so she felt she could make such decisions about him. Old Billy, the ox, didn't mind the tedious job at all. He had helped with the cane grinding for years.

When the time came for the cane grinding, the Ross family always invited everyone close enough to attend. Queenie could hardly wait for everyone to arrive. The Lightfoot children would be there to play with her, as would Min's family. She looked forward to all the attention!

Queenie reminded Sim that they must put aside a nice jar of syrup and a jar of cane juice for Crazy Harry. She would place it by the front gate for Harry to pick up some time in the night. She decided to give him several stalks of the good sugar cane as well. She and her friends loved to chew the sweet cane, and she thought Harry would like it, too.

The cane grinding always took place after enough syrup and sugar was stored for family consumption. The Rosses filled jar after jar and stored them all for future use. When their friends and relatives came, they all brought their own jars to fill with the syrup and the fresh cane juice. After standing around drinking cane juice and buck, everyone settled in the yard and on the porch to pick and sing until late in the afternoon. Some friends had even come up from St. George and Moniac. They would be late getting home, but this was an annual frolic that they always looked forward to.

After everyone had finally left with their jars of syrup and juice, Queenie and Sim took Harry's syrup, juice, and cane down to the front gate. Somehow Queenie sensed that Harry was observing the frolic from the nearby woods. She wished that she could stay up and watch for him, but she knew she would not be allowed to do so. She looked down toward the woods as Sim lead her inside.

"Mr. Harry," she called out, "come and get your good surprises!"

"I don't know if he can hear you, Baby," said Sim.

"Oh, yes, Pa," she assured him. "I'm sure he can."

Early the next morning, Queenie ran out to the gate. The syrup, cane juice, and sugar cane were gone, and on top of the fence post was a beautifully carved smiling bear. It was the largest toy Harry had ever made for Queenie. It stood at least a foot high. The delicate carving made the bear's furry coat look as though she could run her hand through the fur and ruffle it. Queenie was elated. She ran into the house telling everyone to come and see her beautiful bear. Queenie was so proud of it that she carried it everywhere for several days, and it quickly became her favorite toy.

After the cane grinding, the Rosses had many more chores to complete. Pickles, beans, peas, and tomatoes had to be canned for the winter months, and corn had to be dried and husked. Some was stored to feed the animals, and some was ground into corn meal. Peanuts were gathered and dried for future use.

They also had to make repairs to the fence, the barn, and even the house. The men went on several hunting trips, and the meat they brought back was smoked, cured, and stored in the little smoke house. The alligator hides and animal furs had to be cleaned and treated for marketing, and there were always other tasks to be completed on their little farm and on the surrounding swamp land.

They had one milk cow, and the milking was a steady job. They used the fresh milk for Queenie, and the sour milk was churned to make butter and buttermilk. There were several fruit trees to tend, including apple, fig, peach, and pear trees, and much of their fruit was dried and put up for winter.

The Ross family busied themselves, as usual, with these chores while the month quickly passed. Soon it would be time to meet Henry again at his house near Traders Hill. They seldom mentioned the gold as they went about their work, but each person knew that it was never far from their minds.

One day they had a surprise visit from Henry. Luckily, Sim and his father were home when Henry pulled up at the landing. Queenie saw him first and ran down to the boat to meet him. As usual, he brought a nice toy for his little friend.

Sim met his friend outside as he walked up to the house with Queenie. "I hope nothing is wrong, Henry," he said.

"Oh, no, quite the contrary, Sim," said Henry. "I just thought I needed to get away from the bank for a little fishing. Would it be convenient for you to go fishing for an hour or so? I can only stay a while. I want to get back to St. George before dark. I'm planning to stay the night with my friend there and then go on home tomorrow."

Sim knew that Henry usually spent the night at St. George when he came up to fish, and he suggested a good fishing place close by. They invited Sim's father to go along, but Jim was busy with repair work on the barn and excused himself.

As soon as they reached the fishing area, Henry told Sim the news that was the real reason behind his fishing plans. The banker at

Jacksonville was still working on the report of the value of the gold, but in the meantime, a thousand acres of swamp land had come on the market. Many of the people who had originally received property in the land lotteries were simply disposing of it for a very low price. They did not attach any value to this swamp land and felt that it was not worth paying taxes on the property. Henry knew that Sim would have enough money to buy this plot, so he brought along a map of the area and some papers for him to sign. This would clinch the sale until Henry could transfer some of Sim's money to his bank at St. Marys. Sim studied the map and realized that much of this land was under water, but he also knew the value of the trees and the animals on the property. His thoughts were in a whirl as Henry explained the situation. He couldn't believe this was actually happening, but he trusted Henry. If Henry said this was the safe thing to do, then he would do it.

"Now, I know all of this is expensive to you, Henry," said Sim. "I don't know much about business, but I do know that you should be sure to take out plenty to cover your expenses. I do thank you, and I can hardly believe all of this good luck is happening to us."

"I know, Sim. I can hardly believe it myself, but I'm enjoying helping you. I suggest that you deposit most of your money in the Jacksonville bank and transfer small amounts periodically to my bank at St. Marys. Don't worry about my expenses. I'll be making money off of your money when you deposit it in my bank. The reason to keep most of your money in Jacksonville is that in a large bank like that, nobody pays attention to large deposits of money. But I employ several local people, and they would be curious about such a large deposit coming in from someone in the south swamp."

Sim insisted that the deposit be made in both his and Jim's names, and Henry agreed that this was a good idea. Sim knew that his Pa would never use any of the money without his knowledge, but he also knew that this would give Jim a sense of importance that he had never felt before.

Henry still wanted the Ross men to meet him at Traders Hill as planned. He left them feeling quite satisfied with his day's work.

Sim was almost bursting to tell Min and his parents what had transpired, but he decided to wait until after supper when Queenie was in bed. Everyone knew something was up, however. They had noticed the papers Sim had carried back to his bedroom, and his face bore a smile that he couldn't hide. All during supper he talked about everything but land and money, and his family respected his silence on the matter. They knew that he would explain the real reason for Henry's visit when the time was right.

As soon as Queenie was tucked in and fast asleep, he brought out the papers and gathered his family around him. "You won't believe what I'm goin' to tell you, so get prepared for a shock. We are now quite well off, accordin' to Henry." There was no response from anyone, so he continued. "In a short time, we will own a thousand acres of this swamp, in addition to what we already have. It's land that was originally part of the state lottery, and the people who got the land didn't want it. They didn't want to pay taxes on it because they thought it was no good because so much of it is under water. They're lettin' it go for a few dollars an acre."

Jim could hold his tongue no longer. "Good heavens, Son! Didn't they have any idea at all how much these trees are worth? Didn't they realize how much these hides and furs are worth? Didn't they know that this swamp is the prettiest and most restful place on earth?" Jim could simply not accept the fact that others did not realize what he already knew from his many years of living in the swamp.

"No, Pa," answered Sim. "I guess they didn't. You see, most of them have never been down here. All they know is that it's swamp land, and most of it isn't fit for farming as they know it." He paused. "Well, speak up, ladies. What do you think of all this?"

"I'm just too shocked to take it all in," said Aggie.

"Me, too," said Min. "I'm beginning to realize what this can mean for our little girl. Even though we've agreed to be very careful not to let folks know that we've hit a lucky streak, I guess it still means that Queenie will always have everything she could ever want or need in life."

"I know," said Sim. "That's what I've been thinkin', too. Now, I want you all to look at this map that Henry brought. This is where the thousand acres are located. Lots of it is actually dry land and fit for farmin'. The rest is under water most of the time, but that still don't mean that it's worthless."

Sim explained Henry's recommendation that they leave most of their money in the Jacksonville bank for some time and just move a small amount to St. Marys periodically. He explained how Henry would make his money from the deal, then turned to Jim and told him that the money was in a joint account in both of their names.

"On, no, Son. That won't be necessary," said Jim. "I know that whatever either of us has will always be shared."

"It's already done, Pa. Now any time you or Ma needs anything, you can just get the money for it without any trouble. And, of course, Min knows that what's mine is hers, too."

"Don't worry, Sim, me and Miss Aggie will be thinkin' of things to buy," teased Min as she grinned at Aggie.

"Oh, yeah, we'll be doin' that," added Aggie, returning Min's broad smile.

Jim was truly excited. "I think I need a little toddy for my heart after all this excitement," he said.

"I think I'll be joinin' you, Pa. We'll even let our women have some, too."

Aggie and Min seldom joined the men when they had a drink of spirits from Joe Lightfoot's stills, but this time they both decided that they needed some to calm their nerves.

Chapter Six

☾

Everything at the Ross place moved along as usual in the days following Henry's good news about the money and the purchase of the land. The Rosses knew that their finances were vastly improved and that they now owned a great deal of land, but life for them remained the same. The hunting, the fishing, the production of spirits at Joe's stills, and the household chores all remained the same. They didn't even make an immediate shopping trip to Traders Hill. Sim and Mr. Jim knew that they were to meet Henry there in a couple of weeks anyway, so they could do their shopping then.

If they had good weather for their trip, they might even take the women along. Sim especially wanted Queenie to accompany them. She was growing into a very independent little girl. In fact, her parents were having to keep a tight rein on her activities to keep her out of things that could become quite dangerous.

When the time came to go to Traders Hill to meet Henry, Aggie and Min decided to stay home and quilt. Since they had a new quilt pattern, they asked the men to buy new material for them, and they made a list of household items to be purchased as well. Aggie and

Min really didn't want to bump along all the way to Traders Hill in the oxcart. Queenie, however, insisted on going along, so Min placed a pillow in the cart for her to sit on. Queenie also wanted to take a toy along and chose the bear that Harry had given her at the cane grinding. She was very excited about her trip, and the rough ride in the oxcart didn't bother her. She was going to town, and that was enough to ease any pain or discomfort along the way.

They drove directly to Henry's house. He had not yet arrived, so Sim used their key to open the door. Sim and Jim gave Queenie a tour of the farm, and she was so excited that she even left her bear in the cart. She ran through the house looking at the things that were so different from her home in the swamp. Sim and Jim explained why there were no chickens in the yard, why there was no horse there, and why there was no ox or oxcart to go along with the house. It was hard for Queenie to understand why nobody lived in such a pretty house.

When Henry arrived a short time later, Queenie ran out to meet her friend. He was so happy to see her that he promised to take her shopping before they left Traders Hill.

Henry had been able to secure even more land for them—not as much as in the first purchase, but two smaller plots that were deeper in the swamp. These included some small islands, but most of the area was wet land or "trembling earth," which would be valuable for the alligators, fish, and cypress trees it contained.

While the men discussed business, Queenie went out to the oxcart to get her toy bear. She carried it in to show to Henry, but when he saw the beautifully carved bear, he suddenly went pale.

"Where did you get such a beautiful toy, Queenie?" he asked.

"My friend, Mr. Harry, gave it to me. He gives me lots of pretty things he has made."

Henry turned to Sim. "Who is this 'Harry'? Do you know his surname?" he asked.

"I don't rightly know," answered Sim. "Harry is the only name I have ever heard him called."

"Does he live in the swamp?"

Sim explained that Harry was a rather mysterious man who lived somewhere deep in the swamp, but they had never been able to find out where he stayed. Sim described how Harry had come to their house only once—when Queenie was a baby. He told Henry how he had made so many pretty toys for her and explained how they had tried to repay him. "We believe that he knows everything that goes on at our place. We can see him sometimes in the woods near the house when we're pickin' and singin' on our front porch. Pa has hollered out to him to come up and join us, but if we speak to him, he always runs off."

"How does he look? Does he look very old?" asked Henry.

"It's actually hard to tell," answered Jim. "He seems plenty spry, but he has so much beard that you can't rightly tell what he looks like. But his beard is dark, and I reckon if he was very old it would be gray."

Henry sat running his fingers over the life-like bear, and Sim thought he saw tears well up in Henry's eyes. "I know this seems odd," explained Henry, "but I know of only one person who can do this kind of beautiful work. I'm referring to my brother who left St. Marys some years ago with a group of young men headed out west. I can't help wondering if he could have left the group and gone to live in the south swamp. I must find this man. Do you think there is any way I can make contact with him?"

"We've tried to find his livin' place, but we've never had any luck," said Jim. "I do think maybe Joe Lightfoot could help us. He's told me that he sees him over around the stills sometimes. Joe says that he's also seen smoke comin' from deep in Blackjack Island, and he's wondered if that could be where Harry lives. The trouble is that Harry runs when anybody tries to get near him."

"My twin brother's name is Harry, and this all adds up. He probably doesn't know that the war is over and thinks he'd be drafted if he got caught. I just can't bear to think that my brother might be living out there alone. All this time I thought that he was with his friends, safe and sound out west somewhere."

"We'll get in touch with Injun Joe and see if he can help us," volunteered Sim.

"Please do, and as soon as I can make arrangements, I'll come up to your place. Let's get with Joe and see if we can find this man. If he's not my brother, at least I'll know that much," said Henry.

Queenie had taken her toy back from Henry and had gone out to play, so she did not hear the plans that the men made to try to find Harry. Sim was glad they had taught her to call him "Mr. Harry" and not "Crazy Harry." Henry had told them that his brother was slightly retarded, and Sim certainly did not want his child to refer to this man as crazy.

They had settled down to business again and soon called Queenie in to eat the lunch they had brought from home. Before they parted company, Henry asked if he could take Queenie shopping. So while the two of them shopped for toys, Sim and Mr. Jim bought supplies to carry home. Henry had informed them of the balance of their bank account and assured them that they should feel free to buy just about anything they wanted. Swamp residents, however, generally wanted very little and needed very little because almost everything necessary for their livelihood could be found in the swamp and around their homes.

They finished their shopping at Traders Hill and went their separate ways. Sim and Mr. Jim could not help feeling anxious about Henry. He seemed so sure that Harry was his brother, and they feared that he would meet with disappointment if they couldn't find him. They would do their best to help him, however. After all, he had already done so much for them and their family.

Queenie left Traders Hill without a worry in the world. She sat on her pillow in the oxcart and opened one package after another.

"I'm afraid," said Jim, "that Henry is spoilin' that child."

Sim laughed aloud. "Just look who's talkin', Pa."

"I know, but ain't it hard not to spoil that little girl?"

"As usual, you are right, Pa."

The two men should have been overjoyed that Henry had found still more land for them—land so cheap that it was almost like a gift. They were so engrossed in Henry's concern for Harry, however, that they almost forgot about their good luck. In the meantime,

Queenie had fallen asleep on her pillow, hugging her bear and her new toys.

Finally, Sim got his thoughts together and realized how very lucky they were. "We ain't thinkin' straight, Pa. Here we are worryin' about Harry instead of thinkin' how lucky we are. Do you realize that we are buyin' up most of the south swamp? I would say we are well off, and some day we may even be rich."

"That's right, Son, but I just can't seem to take it all in. I come down here from Carolina with nothin', and now just look at us. I guess a body would think we'd be spendin' money like crazy, but there we was in town, and all we bought was things we just had to have."

"Well, Pa, I didn't see anything I really wanted. Did you?"

"Not really. I guess we should've bought somethin' for our women folks besides just some quiltin' cloth."

"Oh, well, Pa, we'll do better next time. I guess we just got too side-tracked by Henry's trouble."

They rode the rest of the way in silence until it was time to make the holler. That woke Queenie from her nap, and she talked constantly all the way home. When they finally arrived back at the homeplace, she gave Aggie and Min a full account of her exciting day at Traders Hill and delighted in showing them her new toys. She went to sleep surrounded by them, but the one she held closest to her was her bear from Mr. Harry.

Within a short time, Sim had gone to see Joe Lightfoot and told him about Henry's dilemma. Joe agreed to help but had some doubts about their plan. "We can get near to him, but he probably will run. Woods are thick on that island. There are many snakes and much boggy land there, too."

"Well, at least we can try to help Henry," said Sim. "He seemed very worried about this man. He feels sure that Harry is his twin brother, and frankly, I'm beginnin' to think so, too."

"I'm glad to help, Sim, but be sure you have plenty bullets for your gun. It's dangerous land there—snakes everywhere and many dangerous animals."

"As long as you'll guide us to the area where you think he's livin', that's the best we can do. We'll bring guns and bullets for protection. We'll let you know as soon as Henry comes up, and all of us can help him as much as possible."

Joe agreed, and Sim returned home to report to Jim what they had decided.

"That's all we can do right now, Son," said Jim. "I do hope it works, though. I'm thinkin' that Harry will not likely be willin' to leave the swamp. He's lived alone so long that he's almost become a wild man. He feels safe out there, wherever he's livin'. He must get enough to eat, because he seems healthy, and he's livin' in a place where he's not in constant fear. If he came into the swamp at the beginnin' of the war, he would've been away from civilized folks for ten or eleven years now. That's a long time to be away from other people."

"I'm afraid that Henry will be in for a bad shock even if we do find Harry," agreed Sim.

They readied their weapons and went about their daily routines as they waited for Henry's visit. They felt that Henry would come soon because he seemed so anxious about his brother. And sure enough, Henry showed up at the Ross place in a matter of days. Sim assured Henry that he, Jim, and Joe would do everything possible to help find Harry.

Henry, Sim, and Jim set out almost immediately for Injun Joe's place. Joe joined the group, and they paddled and poled their way through the swamp water, skirted large patches of trembling earth, and headed straight for the huge Blackjack Island. Joe explained to Henry that he had seen Harry going in that direction and had seen smoke rising from the central part of the island. This, however, was not a sure sign that Harry lived there. There were always renegades who hid out in the swamp to get away from trouble on the outside. For this reason, their mission could be a dangerous one.

When they reached the island, they docked their boat and secured it firmly. Sim had brought along a chain and lock so they could anchor the boat to a large tree. This was necessary because swamp renegades would gladly steal such a good boat.

The four men trudged inland and periodically called out Harry's name. Henry repeatedly identified himself, telling his would-be brother that he wanted to talk to him, that the war was over, and that he wanted him to come home.

As the men went deeper into the trees, they marked their route with white strips of cloth. They knew that a person could easily become lost in the thick undergrowth. Nothing seemed to exist there but snakes that crawled and hung from tress and bears that glared at them and then scampered away when a gun was fired in their direction.

After tramping through the woods and muck for some time, they approached the general area where Joe had seen the smoke. From a distance, they could see a small clearing, in the center of which stood a small shack.

"Be very careful. Let's ease over into that area," said Jim quietly. "This may not be the man we're lookin' for, and people in this swamp are not beyond shootin' a person. I'll give a loud holler before we move that way."

Jim made the holler a couple of times, but there was no answer. He tried again, and when he still received no response, he motioned for the others to follow him. All those years in the swamp had taught him the dangers of catching a person off guard.

Slowly the men moved forward. There was no smoke, no movement around the cabin. As they moved toward the structure, they realized that it was a little larger than they had first thought it to be.

"Maybe it's just a hunter's cabin," said Sim.

He stepped up to walk close to Jim. He must not let anything happen to his Pa. His hand was on his gun, and he knew that he would shoot anyone who threatened them. Slowly they all eased forward.

"I think the cabin is empty," said Joe. "I'm goin' to ease 'round back. You stay here."

Joe carefully crept behind the cabin, then eased around to the front. He stepped noiselessly up to the door, and when he saw that the room was empty, he motioned for the others to follow. The inside of the cabin was dark, but when their eyes adjusted, they could see a crude bed, a table, and one chair. These homemade pieces had definitely been made by a skilled hand.

On the table were some tools, and there was a half-carved animal and some wood shavings on the dirt floor where the house's occupant had apparently been working.

"Good heavens!" exclaimed Henry. "This has to be my brother." Strong man that he was, Henry began to sob. To think that his brother had spent years in this jungle while he and his wife lived in comfort down at St. Marys!

"He may be close by, Henry," said Jim. "If he heard us comin', he might have run off. Maybe he's not too far away. We'll give a call to him, tell him his brother is here, and maybe he'll come back."

They called and called, but there was no response. Finally, Henry went to the edge of the woods, identified himself, and begged his brother to come out and talk. But still there was no response. He gave up and joined the others.

"There's only one other thing I know to do now," said Henry. "He can read a little, so I'll leave a note for him."

In his note, Henry explained in simple terms that the war was over and that they wanted him to come home. He also wrote that he had brought lots of food and some clothes that he would leave with the Ross family. He asked Harry to contact them. They would let Henry know when to come for his brother, if Harry would only agree to come home.

The only thing the men could do was return to their boat and head for the Ross place. Henry left the food and clothes with Miss Aggie and Min, and Sim told him that they would put them where they usually left things for Harry. Sim planned to sit in the dark and guard these supplies until Harry picked them up—no matter how long it took.

Henry spent that night with his friend in St. George, and the following day he returned home to St. Marys. He hoped and prayed that he would soon receive word from his brother.

Chapter Seven

☾

Sim carefully placed the articles that Henry had brought for Harry high up on the fence posts. Up there, they would be out of reach of the hogs, but the bears were another problem. They could easily climb or rear up on their hind feet to reach the articles. Sim knew that they would mainly be after the food. Bears were real scavengers, and sometimes they would attack the Ross's small pigs, as well other livestock. Sim and his father had killed or run off most of the bears in the area, but just in case there were still some left on the island, Sim planned to guard Henry's gifts until Harry came and got them. He hoped that Harry had been able to read Henry's note and would come soon.

Harry did not come the first night after Henry's visit. The second night, however, Sim had very good luck. He sat on the front porch watching the low-hanging moss as it swayed back and forth in the cool evening breeze. He was feeling a bit sleepy when he heard a boat quietly approach the landing. Sim could tell that it was Harry. The moonlight highlighted the outline of the hunched-over, bearded man. Sim wanted to call out to him, but he dared not, because he was almost certain that Harry would run off if he did.

Harry had to make three trips to his boat to load all of the supplies that were waiting for him. After he had loaded the last of the supplies onto his boat, he made one more trip up from the landing. He placed something on the gate post, then returned to his boat. Sim was torn between keeping quiet or running down to the landing to try to stop Harry. Surely Harry had found the note from Henry and would now want to see his brother. Sim, however, decided that he should remain silent for the present. At least they knew where Harry lived, and now he had a good supply of food and clothing.

As soon as the sound of Harry's boat had faded into the distance, Sim went down to see what Harry had left on the gate post. Even in the moonlight, Sim could see that it was a beautifully carved eagle. He carried it inside the house and lit a lamp so he could get a closer look at it. The wings were spread as though in flight, and the delicate carving made the feathers look real. Sim could hardly wait for Queenie to see her new toy.

He went to bed soon thereafter but had trouble getting to sleep. Had he done the right thing by remaining silent? Should he have taken a chance and called out to Harry? He wished one of his parents were awake so that he could ask if he had done the right thing. But he would just have to wait until morning.

When Queenie awoke and found her new toy, she was elated. She had to show it to everyone before she could settle down to eat her breakfast.

Everyone felt that Sim had been wise to remain silent and not risk frightening Harry away. Sim felt better, but he still worried about Harry. He wished Henry would come up soon and advise him on what to do.

For the next week, all was quiet at the Ross place. Early one morning the following week, however, Sim heard a peculiar noise near the front gate. It sounded like someone saying, "Help me, help me!" There were always so many peculiar noises in the swamp that at first Sim thought it might be a bird or an animal of some kind. Nevertheless, he went down to the gate to investigate, and there, sprawled on the ground and writhing in pain, was Harry.

"Pa! Come quick!" Sim yelled. Mr. Jim ran down the front steps and joined Sim and a very sick Harry.

"I think he's been snakebit, Pa," said Sim. "Let's get him inside quick."

When the remainder of the household had been alerted, Aggie took charge and directed the men to help Harry to one of the beds. Queenie insisted that they use her room.

Once Harry was settled, the adults had no trouble confirming that he had been bitten by a poisonous snake. This danger was familiar to all swamp people, and they kept medicine on hand for such emergencies. Whether it was too late to save Harry was another question. Nevertheless, they administered their medication and tried to get Harry to tell them what kind of snake had bitten him and how long ago it had happened. Harry, however, was unable to tell them anything. He had tried to get to his only friends before it was too late, and now these friends must help him if they could. He was already badly swollen, so they knew that the poison had probably saturated his body.

While Aggie forced the medicine into Harry's mouth, Min bathed his hot face and hands. "Pray, everybody. Pray hard for this poor swamp man," said Aggie. "Only God can save him now."

Queenie was hovering near the bed, watching her sick friend fight for his life. Min asked her to leave the room until Harry was better. "No," said Queenie. "I can't go. He's my friend. I must stay and talk to him."

When she saw that Queenie had made up her mind, Min said no more and let her stay in the room. Queenie began to talk to Harry, to tell him she was his friend and that she loved him. She was crying, but her tears did not upset Harry, because he couldn't hear her, or anyone else.

In the meantime, Sim and Mr. Jim had gone into the hall. Sim felt that he should get to St. George as soon as possible and send word to Henry through his friend there. He only hoped that Harry would live until Henry arrived. Jim agreed to remain at home to help the women care for their sick friend.

Soon Sim was on his way, promising to return quickly. He knew that his family would do everything they could to save Harry's life.

Sim had no trouble finding Henry's friend, John Scott, at St. George. John, however, reminded Sim that even though he would leave immediately, it would be at least the following day before he could reach Henry at St. Marys. Sim assured John that he and his family would do everything they could to keep Harry alive. He suggested that perhaps Henry could bring a doctor with him, but if that were not possible, maybe he could at least bring a new supply of medication.

Sim returned home and found Harry still alive, but he seemed to be fighting for every breath. In the meantime, Mr. Jim had gone for Fawn, who knew more about medicines than anyone in the south swamp. When she and her family arrived, she administered the herbs that she hoped would help Harry, and Aggie and Min stood by to give her any assistance they could. Jim had finally convinced Queenie that they needed to go to the kitchen and prepare food for the family. After everyone had eaten, they insisted that Queenie remain in the kitchen instead of constantly standing by Harry's bed. At that point, they were afraid that he might breathe his last at any time, and they didn't want young Queenie to witness Harry's death.

Queenie was finally distracted by Joe Lightfoot and his children. Joe insisted on doing his part to help Harry, and the children were sent outside to play. Queenie cried when she told her friends about poor Mr. Harry. "Harry will be well soon," consoled Pete. "I seen snakebite before. Ma knows what to do to make him well. You'll see."

Dawn added her assurance to Pete's. They both believed that their mother could heal almost any illness. They had seen her work successfully so many times with sick people among their Indian relatives and friends. Nevertheless, Queenie still left her playmates periodically to go in and check on Harry's progress.

The Lightfoot family left around nightfall. Fawn left full instructions about the medication and promised to return early the next morning.

The Ross family took turns attending to Harry throughout the night. Some time before dawn, he showed a slight, temporary improvement. He opened his eyes and saw Sim sitting by the bed. "Sim Ross," he said, but his voice faded away, and he closed his eyes again.

"What is it, Harry?" asked Sim.

Harry opened his swollen eyes again. "Tell Brother thank note, and…." His voice faded away again.

Sim could not wake him again, so he just sat and waited and hoped.

Harry remained unconscious for the rest of the night. He mumbled a few words, but mostly he just moaned as though he were in intense pain. Fawn returned early the next morning and brought more herbs for the sick man. Aggie and Min took turns assisting her.

Around noon, they allowed Queenie in the room to speak to Harry. She took the eagle from the shelf and walked over to the bed. "Mr. Harry," she said, "do you remember this pretty bird you made for me? Open your eyes, Mr. Harry. This is your friend, Queenie."

Slowly Harry opened his eyes. "Little friend, Queenie," he said. "Pretty little Queenie."

He closed his eyes and groaned softly. Queenie patted his hand and left the room. She held her eagle in her small hands and whispered to the bird. "Mr. Harry will get well, won't he, Mr. Eagle?" She made the eagle nod as though it were agreeing with her.

The day dragged on, and toward nightfall a boat pulled up to the landing. Henry had rushed to the Ross place as soon as he could, but the only doctor at St. Marys had already gone to Jacksonville. Henry's friend at St. George had offered to accompany him, but Henry did not know how long he would stay at the Ross home and thought he should go alone. His only wish was to find his brother still alive so he could help him to get well.

Sim met Henry at the landing and gave him the full details of Harry's condition, how he had spoken briefly during the night, what he had said, and his brief response to Queenie. "We're putting much stock in what Joe's wife, Fawn, is doin' for Harry," said Sim. "The

Indians know lots that we don't know about herbs and medicines of the swamp. Ma and Min are tryin' to feed Harry, and he's been able to take a small amount of liquids. That's 'bout all I can tell you, Henry. I just don't know what his chances are."

Henry thanked him and hurried into the house. When he saw his pathetic, heavily bearded, nearly unrecognizable brother, he sobbed. The Ross family quietly left the room, but Fawn remained with her patient. Henry thanked her profusely for all she had done for Harry.

Henry talked to his brother, hoping he could somehow get through to him. There was no response, so Henry sat quietly with his head in his hands. Aggie eased into the room and insisted that he come out for some food and a cup of hot coffee. Henry followed her to the kitchen, and the Ross family and their friend sat around the kitchen table and discussed Harry's condition.

"Fawn thinks he has a fairly good chance," Aggie assured them. "We'll do everything we can to help him. It's a miracle he was able to get to us after the snakebite. We must never give up hope."

Min said, "Now, Mr. Cooper, feel free to use our room, next to Harry's. We can manage just fine on pallets in the sittin' room."

"Thank you, Mrs. Ross. I do want to stay until we know if Harry will get well. It just breaks my heart to see the condition he's in. If he does get well, I must never let him go back to that shack where he was living."

"He's welcome to stay here with us as long as he wishes," said Mr. Jim. "We're all praying that he'll get well."

Henry thanked him. "My wife, Mary, wanted to come up with me, but I thought she should wait there and help tend to the bank while I'm away. I'll forever be grateful to all of you and to Fawn, for taking care of him."

While the adults finished their cups of coffee in the kitchen, Queenie slipped into Harry's room again and asked Fawn's permission to talk to him. She eased over to his bed and took hold of his hand.

"Mr. Harry," she said, "please talk to me. You are my friend, and I love you. Can you hear me, Mr. Harry?"

Queenie waited and stood quietly as she patted the sick man's hand. Suddenly Harry opened his eyes and looked at Queenie.

"Little Queenie," he said. "Harry's little friend."

"Oh, Mr. Harry, you're awake! Tell me how you feel."

"Maybe better, a little better, Queenie."

"Keep talkin', Queenie," said Fawn as she eased out toward the kitchen. "I'll be right back. Keep talkin'."

Fawn went to the kitchen door and motioned for Henry to come with her. Henry jumped up, fearing the worst, and followed Fawn. When he got to the door he heard Queenie's voice and Henry's labored response. "Oh, thank God," said Henry, as he eased over to the bed. Tears ran down his face, and he couldn't speak. He was overcome with emotion.

Queenie moved aside so that Henry could get closer to the bed. Henry regained his composure and said, "Harry, my brother, Harry. Thank God you're better. I am so grateful that you are still alive."

He put his arms around the sick man and kissed his feverish brow. Harry clung to his brother as tears welled up in his eyes. "Thank note, Brother. Thanks food and clothes," mumbled Harry. "Very sleepy now."

The Ross family had eased into the adjoining room and heard this exchange. Queenie joined her parents and grandparents. She did not like to see anyone cry, so she asked, "Why are they cryin', Ma? I thought they would be happy that Mr. Harry is better."

"Oh, they are happy, Honey. They're cryin' from happiness," answered Min.

"I thought people cried when they got hurt or when they was sad."

"This is a different kind of cryin', a good kind of cryin'," said Min.

The Ross family quietly left Fawn and the two men alone. As Queenie followed her father out of the room, she could not understand why Henry was so concerned about Harry. "Pa," she asked, "how does Mr. Henry know Mr. Harry? I thought Mr. Henry lived way down there at St. Marys."

Sim suddenly realized that they had neglected to tell Queenie that the two men were brothers. He took her aside and explained the situation.

"Oh, Pa," said Queenie when Sim had finished, "we have to help Mr. Harry get well so he can go home with his brother!"

"That's right, Baby," he replied. "We have to help him."

Henry accepted the invitation to remain at the Ross place until Harry recovered. Harry did improve very slowly, and after three days Henry felt that he could safely return to St. Marys for a few days. Fawn assured him that he need not worry. She would continue to help Aggie and Min take care of Harry. She advised him, however, that Harry should not be moved for several weeks. Henry trusted her judgment after he had seen the good care that she had given his brother, and he insisted on paying her for her services. She refused the money, but Henry left some for her anyway. He offered money to the Ross family, but he knew that they would not accept it.

Harry insisted that he go back to his little shack as soon as he was well. Henry did not argue with him, but he knew that never again would he allow his brother to face the dangerous elements in the swamp alone.

"Don't want to go to St. Marys, Brother," Harry told Henry. "People laugh at me, call me 'Crazy Harry.'"

"I won't allow them to tease you, Harry," Henry assured him. "Mary wants you to come home so we can help you get well. Anyway, if you don't want to stay there, when you are strong again you can live in the house that I bought up near Traders Hill."

"I want my tools and my table so I can carve toys for little Queenie," said Harry.

"Now, don't worry about any of that. Sim, Mr. Jim, Joe, and I will get all of your belongings when I come back."

"Don't know. I'll think 'bout it," said Harry.

Henry left the Ross place feeling that Harry would be well enough to come home soon. His brother's recovery was a miracle. At Fawn's advice, Henry decided to wait at least two weeks before he returned for his brother.

"He needs much food and nourishment now," Fawn told him. "He's still very weak, but he'll be well soon."

Sim promised that he, Mr. Jim, and Joe would retrieve Harry's belongings from his shack one day soon. He also promised to accompany the two brothers as far as St. George when Henry returned for Harry. That way, they would have an extra boat for Harry's belongings, and Henry's boat could be made more comfortable for Harry to ride in. Even with Harry's recent improvement, they knew that he would not regain his full strength for a long time.

A few days later, the Ross men and Joe Lightfoot crossed the south swamp to Harry's shack. After Harry's snakebite, they were all extremely careful. They salvaged what food and clothing that was worth saving and packed up Harry's tools and work table. Sim could not leave the homemade chair. It was a work of art, and he could only imagine the hours that Harry had spent building that piece of furniture. He loaded the chair along with the other articles, and the men headed home.

Harry was like a little child when he saw his possessions. "I start carving soon," he said. "Little Queenie like to have chair I made?"

"Oh, yes, Mr. Harry. It's so pretty!" she answered. She hugged Harry and immediately ran over and sat in her new chair.

"Little Queenie look pretty in chair I made," said Harry. "I make more chairs sometime."

As Harry improved, he resumed his carving. He made animals and toys for Queenie and for the Indian children. Dawn and Pete were often at the Ross place, and Harry became very fond of them, too.

Queenie spent much of her time with Harry, and Sim was shocked one day to hear her ask Harry a question that was much too personal. "Mr. Harry," she asked, "why don't you cut your hair and shave your beard like Pa does?"

"Don't know why, little Queenie. Think I should do that?" he asked.

"Oh, yes. Pa will cut your hair and shave you if you want him to."

Sim was too shocked to speak. They had not taught Queenie to be so disrespectful of adults. But before Sim could correct her, Harry was asking him to help him cut his hair and shave. There was nothing Sim could do but comply. By that time Harry was sitting up, and Sim knew that the exertion of the barbering would not hurt him.

When they were finished, Queenie jumped up and down, clapping her hands. "Mr. Harry, you look so good," she said, handing him the mirror so he could see himself.

"This way I looked when I left St. Marys long time ago, very long time ago," he said. "Brother be surprised when he come."

"You're sure right there, Harry. You look like a new man," said Sim.

Harry was happy to receive so much attention. The Lightfoot family paid him several visits, and he thanked Fawn over and over for helping him to get well. He had begun to eat quite well, and he even drank a small amount of the spirits that Joe had brought over. When he saw how proud Dawn and Pete were of their carved animals, he worked hard and made more toys for them and for Queenie as well.

Soon it was time for Harry's brother to return, and Henry could not believe his eyes when he saw his brother clean-shaven and sporting his new short haircut. Sim assured Henry that Queenie was responsible for the change.

"This is the way you looked when you left home, Harry," said Henry. "This makes me feel that you're really back with us now. Mary is so happy that you are coming home," he added.

"Love Sister Mary, but don't want to leave Ross friends," said Harry.

"Don't worry, Brother. We'll be coming back here to visit our friends," assured Henry.

All of the family walked down to the landing with them when they left. Henry had made a very comfortable seat for Harry in his boat, and Sim followed with Harry's belongings in one of the Ross boats. The little group stood at the landing and waved to Harry until both boats were out of sight.

"Thank God," said Mr. Jim, "that we were able to pay back Henry in a small measure for what he has done for us. We're sure goin' to miss Harry, though."

"'Specially me, Grandpa," said Queenie. "We had such a good time with him while he was here. I hope he comes back soon." Queenie wiped away a small tear with the back of her hand.

Chapter Eight

☾

Queenie did miss Harry, and the Indian children seemed to sense this. They made a point to come over more often, and Queenie was given more liberty to leave the island with them for short excursions. They fished but were not allowed to go hunting. Sim planned to teach Queenie how to use a gun, but that could come later when she was older.

As Queenie grew older, her delicate features and blond curls did not quite match her athletic body. She was as strong and agile as her Indian playmates. When her friend Dawn reached her teenage years, she grew into a very beautiful young woman. Her dark beauty contrasted Queenie's blonde prettiness, and the two girls became close friends in spite of the difference in their ages.

Dawn's brother Pete usually felt obliged to protect the two girls when they all played together. If they were out in the boat, he gave orders and decided where they would go and where they would be safe. The two girls sometimes argued against his decisions, but they usually ended up doing as he said.

"I tell you this," he said stubbornly, "if you don't mind me, I'll not take you out to fish again. Dawn knows not to disobey me, but the same must go for you, Queenie."

"But I ain't your sister, Mr. Pete Lightfoot," responded Queenie.

"You're my sister when you're in my boat," he retorted. "Remember, if you want to go again, you have to do as I say. I told Mr. Sim that I'd take care of you, and that's what I'll do."

Queenie knew he was right, so she finally consented to following his directions. When they returned from their outing, however, she complained to her Pa.

"He's right, Honey," Sim told her. "He's older than you are, and he's had more experience in these swamps. I'm glad for you to have playmates, but you must listen to Pete when you are out with the him."

Queenie was not quite sure that she agreed with Pa, but she knew that children did not question the judgment of their parents. Besides, she felt sure that Pete would keep his word about not taking her fishing if she argued with him, and she did love to go fishing with her friends.

Queenie not only became good at fishing, but she also began to catch small animals to keep as pets. Sim and Mr. Jim kept busy building pens for a little bear, several wounded birds, a pet squirrel, and even a small doe. Queenie spent hours feeding them, talking to them, and nursing the wounded ones back to health. Dawn and Pete helped her tend to them and supplied most of their names.

Every few weeks, Henry gave the Rosses good reports of Harry's progress. After he regained his health, Harry decided to live in the house near Traders Hill. Sim promised Henry that he would take Queenie over to see Harry as soon as he was settled in his new home.

Henry also informed them that Harry had recently done so well with his carving and woodwork that he was quickly developing a good market for his products. He was now building chairs, tables, and other pieces of furniture, and many of the new people moving into St. Marys were asking for Harry's handmade pieces faster than he could fill the orders. Harry felt that he could work better in the quietness of the house near Traders Hill, and Henry understood. Harry promised never again to enter the swamp alone. He had learned his lesson from the near deadly snakebite. He did look forward, however, to visiting his friends in the south swamp.

Once Harry was settled in, Sim and Jim were unable to go see Henry or go shopping at Traders Hill without Queenie going along. She always wanted to visit her friend, Mr. Harry, and he regularly gave her a new, beautifully carved toy. He built a little dresser for her room and later made her a pretty little rocking chair to match.

Each time Henry went to Traders Hill, Harry had several pieces of furniture ready for him to carry down to St. Marys or Traders Hill. These were happy times for Harry. He had friends, and he was making his own living. He felt important for the first time in his life.

Life for Harry's friends in the south swamp moved along as usual. Even though Henry continued to purchase land for them, they still did not feel particularly well-off. They were grateful that they had cash for essentials, but life as they had always known it changed very little. They hunted, fished, farmed, and maintained their home. They attended church and neighborhood gatherings. This was the life they wanted—nothing more.

When Sim felt that Queenie was old enough, he began teaching her to use his gun. She learned fast and could soon handle the gun almost as well as the men in the family. Sim cautioned her of the dangers of handling a gun because, as usual, she seemed afraid of nothing.

Soon Queenie's parents began to allow her to use one of the boats so she could fish in the run in front of their place. They told her to keep in sight of the house at all times and never venture out to the big lake. Queenie was a strong swimmer, but the lake was so infested with lilies, vines, and alligators that if her boat should go from under her, there would be little hope of swimming to safety.

One bright sunny day, Queenie went down the run a short way to fish. But no fish were biting, so after a while, she decided to move farther down the run. Soon she was poling her way into the big lake.

"Oh well," she said aloud. "Pa won't miss me for a little while. They're all tied up with the fence work in the back yard."

She ventured slowly on. Here the fish were biting, and her exhilaration over the growing pile of fish she was catching made her forget her surroundings. She did not even notice the quickly darkening sky until a sudden downpour hit her. When her boat began to rock with the wind and fill up with rain, she grabbed a can from the boat and tried to bail out the water. But it was useless—still the water came, and soon the boat began to sink. She tried to paddle toward some trees along the shore but soon realized that she could not reach them. She knew that she would not be able to swim the distance and that her boat was going down.

Her only hope was a small sapling about twenty feet away. She could probably swim that far, but what then? Nobody would hear her if she hollered, and anyway, Pa must not know what she had done. She would have to figure out some way to get out on her own. Plunging into the lake, she picked her way through the undergrowth in the water and finally reached the sapling. She grabbed the tree's young trunk and hung on as the rain beat against her.

"If the lightnin' don't strike me," she said to herself, "I can hold on a long time. Oh, if Pa catches me, he'll really tan my hide!"

It was not that simple, however. She could hear the heavy grunt of a big alligator in the distance, and even worse was the water moccasin now swimming quickly toward her. Queenie scaled the young tree as far as she could. She kicked at the snake, but he stubbornly remained at the base of the tree. She began to scream, but her voice was barely audible above the thunder and pouring rain.

After a few terrified moments, Queenie realized that a boat was coming toward her. As it came closer, she recognized her friend Pete. "Snake! Snake, Pete!" she screamed as she pointed frantically to the moccasin.

Pete raised his gun and blasted the snake to bits. He jumped into the water and hurried to the Ross boat, nearly completely under water by now. He reached it and managed to bring it up. In the meantime, Queenie still clung to the sapling. She did not ask for Pete's help. She knew that he would give her a piece of his mind for what she had done, because he was quite familiar with the rules Queenie's parents had laid down for her.

"Get down and get into my boat, Queenie," he ordered. "I hope your Pa tans your hide for this stupid thing you've done."

"You ain't gonna tell on me, are you, Pete? You've saved the boat, and you can just take me back to the run, and I'll be all right. They won't know the difference."

"No, I'll not tell on you," Pete replied gruffly. "You tell on yourself. Your punishment will be less that way. But, if you *don't* tell, I will. You stubborn, naughty girl. You need good spanking. I'd do it myself, but maybe Mr. Sim will do a better job."

"Thank you for helpin' me, Pete, but you are a hateful boy! You could've let that snake bite me and finish me off! Then at least you wouldn't have to look after me all the time!"

"Maybe that's what I should have done. Now get in this boat, naughty girl!"

Queenie climbed into Pete's boat, and they headed toward the Ross run, pulling Queenie's retrieved boat behind them.

When they reached the run, they saw Sim poling his way toward them. Queenie recognized the anxiety on his face, and her heart sank as she realized the fright she had caused her Pa.

"I'll be goin' now, Mr. Sim," said Pete. "I'm needed at home. Queenie'll tell you about her bad luck in the rain cloud."

With that, Pete left. He wanted no part of Queenie's punishment. He hoped Mr. Sim would not be too hard on her, but the worried expression on his face spoke volumes. No, Pete did not think Mr. Sim would be too easy on his daughter.

Queenie took a deep breath and told her father the whole story. When she had finished, she said, "Now, I know you're gonna tan my hide, and I know I deserve it, Pa. I just wasn't thinkin' too straight, I guess."

"I don't guess that's what I'll do, Queenie," said Sim. "That's too easy over with. But you won't put your foot in another boat for one whole month, except to go with us to church."

"Oh, Pa, please give me a tannin' instead! I have to go fishin' with my friends."

"No," said Sim firmly. "That's the way it will be. You've got to learn the dangers of the swamp if you want to stay alive, and I aim to do my best to see that you do."

Sim stuck to his word. No amount of coaxing from his wife or his parents could convince him to reduce her punishment. He did feel a little guilty on the occasions when Queenie went down to the landing and just stood quietly, looking at the boats.

Dawn and Pete came over often to visit, but they did not mention going fishing. They knew the whole story and had no intention of interfering.

Meanwhile, Queenie's family went out of their way to thank Pete for rescuing her, but Pete always shrugged off their gratitude. "She must learn to mind her parents," Pete said simply. "The swamp is a very dangerous place. But I think she'll not do that again."

When Queenie's month-long punishment was finally over, the three children celebrated with a day of fishing. They were allowed to go to the big lake as long as Pete was in control of the boat. Aggie and Min made a big picnic lunch for them, and they happily set off on their adventure. Secretly, however, Sim and Mr. Jim were planning a little trip of their own that would enable them to keep a fairly close eye on the children. Sim realized that he was an overprotective parent, but he couldn't help himself. He knew that Queenie was getting older now, but she was still his only baby.

As they acquired more land, Sim and his family began to sell off some of the timber from the extreme southern part of the swamp. Every year more railroads eased north from Jacksonville and from St. Marys, and the demand was high for timber for this construction. Timber was certainly something the Ross family could supply, and they made good money from its sale. Sim and Mr. Jim did not really need to sell alligator hides or spirits, but they continued to do so because it was a way of life for them. The money in their account at Henry's bank kept growing, but they thought little of this. They had the kind of life they wanted, and money played only a small part in that life.

Their lives were filled with the yearly cane-grinding, the monthly meetings at Bethel Church, the alligator hunts, the shipping of spirits down to Florida, the happy hours of picking and singing on the front porch, and the visits to Traders Hill to meet Henry and visit Harry. They bought new plows, new tools, and a few articles for their home, but as for any real luxuries, they simply were not interested. The did splurge enough to buy a new horse, because Bob was getting so old.

As the years passed, more visitors came to the swamp. The lumber companies brought in many people, white and black, who had been misplaced by the Civil War. These people found the swamps a good place to hunt and fish and began to venture deeper into the area. Some of these people were welcome, and some were not. Some were too daring and went too deep into the swamp and never came out. Sim tried to caution those he met, but many who did not heed his warnings often met with disaster or simply were unable to find their way out. A stranger could go in circles for days and never find his way to safety.

In 1875, Mr. Jim considered giving up the stills. He no longer needed the money from the sale of spirits, but he did not want to take away Joe Lightfoot's main source of income. He wished someone would buy the stills and keep Joe in charge of the enterprise. He mentioned this to a young man from St. George who worked in the south swamp for a lumber company. This young man came into the area often to hunt and fish, and he, Sim, and Jim had become friends. He enjoyed visiting Joe's stills with the Ross men and often carried a good supply of spirits back to St. George with him. The high grade of these spirits invariably pleased his friends.

This young man, Sam Smith, was immediately interested in buying the stills. He had saved most of his money from the lumber camp and made Jim a good offer. Jim accepted and was glad to get the stills off his hands, even though he did occasionally miss his trips over to the river.

Sam Smith and Joe had no trouble adjusting to the new partnership. Sam brought out the sugar and other supplies needed for making the spirits and then hauled the finished product down to Jacksonville. He seemed to enjoy the company of the Lightfoot family as much as that of the Ross family. He particularly enjoyed the young Lightfoot children. They helped him load the spirits into his boat, and he often stayed for a meal with his new Indian friends. Sam had to admit that keeping his eyes off the beautiful daughter of the family was difficult. He realized that Dawn was quite young, but he thought he had never seen such a graceful or beautiful human being.

Fawn Lightfoot noticed Sam's obvious admiration of her daughter, and she also noticed that Dawn seemed very aware of Sam's presence when he visited their home. It was difficult for Fawn to admit to herself that Dawn was no longer a child. She still spent much of her time fishing and roaming the swamps with Pete and Queenie, but her attractively developed body was no longer that of a child. She had become a radiant young woman. Her dark skin, her flowing black hair, and her perfect features were enough to attract the attention of any young male, whether he was white or Indian. Fawn accepted these facts, but she still kept a very close eye on this young man when he was around. She felt that Sam was trustworthy but realized that they actually knew very little about him. The fact that he was a friend of the Ross family was in his favor, and he appeared to be a gentleman. He treated Fawn and her husband with respect and was polite at all times. But still she wondered why he was in St. George in the first place, so far away from his own family. Was he running away from something or someone? But for all her curiosity, Fawn knew she would just have to be patient and wait until Sam Smith told them more about himself.

Chapter Nine

☾

Fawn did not have to wait very long to learn the truth about Sam Smith. He and Dawn soon declared their love for each other, and even though Sam did not know the procedure for asking permission to marry an Indian girl, he planned to proceed as he would among his own people. He told Dawn that he would ask for her hand in marriage, but he must first divulge his true identity and his background to her family. Dawn knew this was best, but she also understood Indian culture. Hers was a proud race of people, and she was afraid that her parents would try to keep her from marrying this handsome white man. He had revealed his identity and his past to her, and still she loved him. But she knew that Sam wanted to explain himself to her parents, and Dawn feared they would not be so willing to accept him.

They all enjoyed a good meal at the Lightfoot home after a new supply of spirits had been loaded onto Sam's boat. The world around them was quiet and at peace, but Sam was nervous. What would he do if Dawn's parents refused to allow their marriage? He had been dwelling on that thought for days. But now he must make his move; for better or for worse, he must know their decision. He only hoped and prayed that they would believe him, as had Dawn.

"My friends," he began, "I have several things I need to tell you. To begin, I want to say that Dawn and I love each other, and we want to be married. But I cannot ask you for her hand in marriage until I tell you who I really am and why I'm here."

Not a person moved. The soft breeze stilled as if to listen, and all was quiet. Sam continued. "My real name is Ben LaFlour. It is true that I come from a good family, but I had some trouble and had to get away, because my life was in danger. My people are sawmillers, and I had a good job in a mill back home. The owner of this mill had a son who stayed drunk most of the time. We did not get along, and we got in a fight one night. He pulled a knife on me, and as I tried to protect myself, he fell on the knife and was killed. I did not kill him. I have never killed anyone. But his father did not believe me. He blamed me for his son's death and vowed to kill me.

"Before he could find me, I managed to escape. I have used an assumed name because, even now, I believe that he is looking for me. I hope you will believe me and keep my secret. Some day I hope to be able to use my real name and know that I am no longer a hunted man.

"I know that I have no right to ask Dawn to become a part of my life under these circumstances, but we love each other so very much.

"If you consent to our marriage, we'll go down to Jacksonville to marry so that I can use my real name on our marriage certificate. She would become Mrs. Benjamin Laflour, and we would live in my little house at St. George. We would ask one or both of you to accompany us to Jacksonville."

For several minutes, neither of Dawn's parents spoke. Then Fawn took the initiative. "I do believe what you say, my friend, but this is a serious matter. Indians should marry Indians. We are a proud race, same as you. Children should be all Indian or all white."

Dawn began to cry softly and moved to Sam's side. For the first time in her life, Fawn saw real hurt in her daughter's eyes. All were quiet for several moments until Joe finally spoke.

"There is another point to consider," he said. "Before too many moons pass, we will travel to the Everglades to join our families. We would not want to leave without our daughter."

Now there were tears in Sam's eyes, too. "We will not marry without your consent. But if you can see fit to give us your blessing, I promise to take good care of her. I am making good money now, and I'll give her a good home. I promise this to you with all my heart."

His voice broke at this point, and he could not go on. Feeling compassion for the young man, Fawn spoke up. "We want a happy life for our daughter. She deserves a good life with a good man. I know you are a good man. So if Joe agrees to go to Jacksonville with you, I will give my blessing."

Dawn ran to her mother, hugged her, and turned to her father. "Is it all right, Pa? Will you go with us?"

"I will go, little papoose," he answered. "I am sad, but I will go."

Pete had not said a word throughout the entire conversation but sat still as a stone. When his parents gave their consent, he jumped to his feet and ran from the house. He knew that the remainder of his life would be spent away from his beloved sister. That was more than he could handle at his young age.

"Pete will be all right soon," explained Fawn. "It will take time for him to realize that his sister must have a happy life with the man she loves."

Joe brought out some spirits, and they drank to the upcoming marriage and planned a date for the trip to Jacksonville. Fawn allowed Dawn to partake of the spirits for the first time. Now that Dawn was about to be married, Fawn realized that she must begin treating her daughter as an adult.

"I'll spend the day with Miss Aggie when you go to Jacksonville," said Fawn to her daughter. "Pete will go with me to talk to Queenie. She will be lonesome, too, now that you are leaving us."

So the decision had been made. Sam would marry the beautiful Indian girl, and the Lightfoot family would move to the Everglades without her.

Soon Fawn paid a visit to Miss Aggie. She sought her advice as well as her consolation, and she knew that Miss Aggie would help her secure some material for a new wedding dress for Dawn.

When she told Aggie and Min about the wedding, they were both shocked. "She's so young, Fawn!" exclaimed Aggie. "And we know so little about this young man."

"That is true," answered Fawn, "but Indian girls usually marry young. Dawn is the same age I was when I married Joe. And we also know a little more about Sam now. He told us about his family, where he is from, and why he is here in the swamp. I cannot tell you what he said, but we think everything will be all right. I'm just sad because my child is about to marry and leave our family. We plan to go to the Everglades to live some day, and we hate to leave Dawn here in Georgia."

Aggie and Min completely sympathized with their friend. Min realized that she was fortunate because she could see her family anytime she wanted by simply crossing the south swamp. Aggie, on the other hand, knew what it was like to be separated from one's family. She missed her family and had never quite forgiven herself for the pain she must have caused her mother.

Min remembered that she had a very pretty length of cloth that she had planned to use for a new dress for herself. She suggested that Fawn use this for Dawn's wedding dress. When she brought out the material and offered it, Fawn was so happy that tears ran down her cheeks. She promised to send Dawn over the following day so her friends could measure her for the dress.

Pete had come to the Ross home with his mother. He and Queenie were out playing with her animals when he told her the news that Dawn would soon be married. Queenie did not believe him. She thought he was making a joke, but when he began to cry, she knew he was serious. Between sobs, Pete managed to tell her the whole story. Queenie then began to cry, too.

Soon Sim came up from the garden. "What on earth ails you two?" he asked. When they told their story between sobs, Sim said, "Now, just hush up your cryin', both of you. Don't you want Dawn to be happy? She loves this young man. I've seen this comin' for some time. You think Dawn is still a child, but that is not true. She's a young woman now, and Sam is a good man.

"The best thing for you two right now is to go and get a couple of fishin' poles. Go out in the run and catch some good, fresh fish for supper. Is your Ma inside, Pete?"

Pete nodded, and Sim hurried into the house. He had to learn the truth of the situation. Was everything all right? Would there be trouble over this interracial marriage? He certainly hoped not, because all these people were his friends, including Sam.

After he heard the story from Fawn, Sim was much relieved. There seemed to be no trouble, just sadness about their losing their daughter. To reassure Fawn, he told her that he believed Sam to be a good, reliable young man.

Dawn and her mother spent the following day at the Ross place. The wedding dress was soon ready, and as Queenie watched Dawn try on the finished garment, she thought she had never seen her friend look so pretty. She had finally decided that Dawn's getting married was all right. She knew that she would miss her friend, but she also knew that they would still be able to visit from time to time.

On the day of the wedding, Joe and Dawn set out for St. George to meet Sam. The trip went well, and when they returned to St. George after the wedding, Joe left the two young people in Sam's comfortable little house. Joe thought that perhaps this was the way life was meant to be and that all people were the same, regardless of their race or the color of their skin. As he paddled home to his family in the deep swamp, he decided one thing for certain—he would wait for a while to join his family and friends in the Everglades. He had hoped to leave within a few months, but now he would wait until at least a year passed to be sure that his daughter's marriage worked out well. He would continue to run the stills as long as they remained in Georgia, because each time Sam came out for a load of spirits, Dawn would come with him. For these short visits at least, their family would be together again.

As the months passed, the Lightfoot family and the Ross family adjusted to Dawn's living down at St. George. She and Sam visited both families often, and it was generally a happy time for all. There was no doubt that the marriage was working well.

Sim knew that Pete missed his sister, because as time passed, he and the Indian boy became close friends. Sim invited Pete to go with him on alligator hunts and fishing trips. He knew that his young friend would likely be going to Florida soon, so he enjoyed his company while he could. Sometimes he took the boy to Traders Hill so that Pete could learn the ways of the outside. On these trips he sometimes even gave him small amounts of money to spend.

On one of the brief visits to the Ross homestead, Sam and Dawn announced that Dawn was going to have a baby. Dawn's family was excited and naturally began making plans for the big event. When the time drew near for the baby to come, Fawn would make one of her rare trips to the outside so that she could be with her daughter.

Fawn admitted to Aggie and Min that she was concerned because Dawn was so young. She said that she herself had been quite young when Dawn was born, and that the birth had been difficult. Maybe Dawn would not have the same trouble, but her mother could not help but worry.

Fawn carefully assembled all of her medicines and prepared herself for the trip to St. George. Joe and Pete accompanied her but returned home after a short visit with Dawn and Sam. This was women's business, and all they could do was wait. The waiting was difficult, but they kept busy to try to free themselves from worry.

After Fawn had been with her daughter for several days, she saw the happiness that existed between Dawn and Sam and realized how excited they were about the coming event. Fawn could not help but feel some of the same joy.

A few days later, Dawn went into labor. It was too soon, and Dawn was very frightened. Fawn did everything she could to calm her, and Sam went for the local doctor, Jim Davis.

When the doctor arrived, Fawn could tell that he was worried, too. He immediately went to work on the suffering young woman. He and Fawn worked tirelessly for a couple of hours, and suddenly the baby arrived.

When Sam saw his beautiful baby boy, he was overcome with emotion. He just knew everything was going to be all right, but that was not to be. Fawn took care of the baby and made him comfortable, but she knew all was not well. Her beloved daughter had lost consciousness. She tried to awaken her and tell her about the baby, but Dawn's pale features let everyone know that she was losing too much blood.

The doctor called to Sam and told him that his wife was critical. "Her mother and I are doing all we can to stop the bleeding, but nothing is working."

"Oh, dear God," Sam sobbed. "Have I killed my precious little Dawn? We both wanted the baby, but maybe it was wrong! Maybe we should have waited. Oh please, please, God, don't let her die!"

He was on his knees by the bed, holding his wife to him, but it was clear to everyone that Dawn was dying. Fawn sobbed aloud, and even the doctor shed tears. A few minutes later, Dawn was gone. Sam remained on his knees with his dead wife in his arms, and Fawn kissed her daughter goodbye and went to the baby. The doctor joined her, examined the baby, and assured her that he was a healthy child.

"Poor little papoose. Doctor Davis, he must live forever without a mother," sighed Fawn.

"Yes, I know, Mrs. Lightfoot, but his Pa will take good care of him. He's a fine man, and he will be all right soon. I know you will help him all you can."

Fawn assured him that she could be depended upon to help. Sam, through his sobs, thanked his mother-in-law and the doctor. He asked the doctor to send word to his close friend, John Taylor, who could send word to Dawn's father and brother. Doctor Davis sent his wife, Mary, and one of her friends to help make funeral arrangements, and John Taylor was soon on his way to deliver the sad news to Joe and Pete. He was instructed to stop by the Ross place as well and tell them the heartbreaking news.

Dawn's family, the Rosses, and members of the Davis's church attended the funeral the following day. They laid Dawn to rest in the little church cemetery at St. George.

The stunned Ross family returned to their home in the south swamp. Dawn's death seemed like a very bad dream. They knew that the Lightfoot family would almost certainly be leaving soon, now that Dawn was gone. They wondered how they would ever adjust to life without their Indian friends.

A grieving Joe and Pete returned to their home but left Fawn with her son-in-law and his baby. She would remain as long as Sam needed her. She hoped that he would agree for her to keep the baby and rear him in the Everglades with their Indian kindred, but she would not suggest this until later.

She noticed that Sam adjusted to fatherhood well. He could handle the infant and care for him without any trouble. When she mentioned this, Sam explained that he had a younger brother and three younger sisters. He had helped his mother tend to them and felt at ease with babies and young children. Fawn could see that Sam loved his baby very much. She thought her heart would break when she watched him spend hours every day at the little cemetery.

Finally, Fawn knew that she must talk with Sam about the baby's future. "We will go to the Everglades soon now. I hope that you will allow us to take the baby and raise him in South Florida. It is too difficult for a man to take care of a baby alone. I promise to take care of him and love him always."

"I do thank you, Mother Fawn, and I know you would take good care of him, but I want to watch him grow up, and I want to do all I can for him. I've been thinkin' about this, and I do know that a small baby needs a woman's care. So as soon as he is a few weeks old, I hope to take him to my Ma. She and the rest of my family can take care of him while he is so small, and then I'll bring him back here to live with me. He is the only part of Dawn that I have left, and it makes me sad to part with him for even a little while." Sam buried his head in his hands, and tears ran down his face as he sobbed.

Fawn was crying too, but she gave him a calming answer. "I am glad that you love the baby so much. I think it is right for you to keep him. I hope to see him again some day. I know it may be a long time, but some day. I'll stay here until you are ready to take the baby to your family. I can help get him strong for the trip. Now, you really must give him a name. What will it be?"

Sam had not thought much about a name, but together they decided he would be Joseph LaFlour, and they would call him "Little Joe." They agreed that Dawn would have liked the name.

Before too long, Joe and Pete were back at St. George. They remained until Sam was ready to leave and take the baby to his family. Fawn carefully packed everything that the baby would need and instructed Sam to stop at farm houses to buy milk for the baby. She felt that Sam and his baby would be all right. When they parted, however, she shed uncontrollable tears. She knew that she would probably never see her grandson again.

After the sad goodbyes to Sam and Little Joe, the Lightfoot family headed home to begin preparations for their long trip to the Everglades in South Florida.

Chapter Ten

☾

The weeks following Dawn's death were sad for the Ross family as well as for the Lightfoots. Joe and Pete spent much of their time at the Ross home waiting for Fawn to return from Sam's house in St. George.

"As soon as Fawn comes home, we go to the Everglades," Joe told his friends. "There's no need to wait now. Sam will take the baby to his family soon, and Fawn will come home then."

"None of us will ever get over Dawn's death," said Aggie. "But we must always remember how happy she was while she was with Sam. I just wish she could have seen her baby and known how fine he was."

"I wish that, too," said Joe, and then he smiled. "They named him Joe, after me. He'll be a good boy always. I'll probably never know for certain, but I hope so."

Queenie and Pete spent most of their time together just talking and trying to understand. Dawn's death was their first real sorrow. They talked and cried freely, and still they could not understand.

"What's bad, too, Pete," lamented Queenie, "is that we'll soon be losing you, too. Your Pa says you'll soon be goin' to the Everglades. I don't guess we will ever see you again once your family leaves. I won't have nobody to play with or go fishin' with. It just don't seem right somehow."

"I know, Queenie, but I can't do nothin' 'bout it," replied Pete. "The government says that Indians were supposed to leave this area a long time ago. Someday I'll have my own family to keep the Indian race goin'. Many of the Indians are goin' to South Florida. There's a big reservation developing down there. People are trying to keep the proud ways of Indians alive."

Queenie did not quite understand why the Lightfoots had to leave Georgia. She believed that all people should be able to live wherever they pleased. What if the government should tell her family they had to leave their home in the south swamp? Well, she simply would not leave; no one could force her to go.

When Joe and Pete went down to St. George to bring Fawn back home, Aggie insisted that they stop by for a meal on their way back. When they arrived, Fawn described Sam's love for his baby and his plans to take Little Joe to his family. She explained that Sam would bring his son back home as soon as the child was a little older. Everyone knew that the days ahead would be difficult for Sam, so the Rosses promised to help him in any way they could.

Sim and Mr. Jim offered to help the Lightfoot family on their journey to the Everglades. They would take extra boats to help get them as far as St. George, but Sim knew that the Indian family would have no means of transportation after they left St. George. Walking from St. George to the Everglades would take a heavy toll on Joe and Fawn. Pete was young and strong, but his parents were getting along in years. So, to help make the Lightfoots' journey easier, Sim and his father purchased a horse and wagon from a company in St. George.

The Indian family could not believe their good fortune. They had no idea that the Rosses had that kind of money to spare. They insisted that they could not accept this offer.

"It's already done, my friends," said Mr. Jim. "We've been sellin' some timber to the sawmill people and have some extra money. We're so happy to help you any way we can. The horse and wagon are yours to keep."

"I can never thank you enough, my friends," answered Joe, as Fawn quietly shed tears of gratitude.

Aggie and Min prepared an ample meal for the two families to share. They ate in virtual silence. There was so much to remember and so much to think about. In spite of their sadness over the loss of Dawn and their anxiety over leaving their home in the swamp, the Lightfoot family felt that everything in the world could not be wrong. When there were still people as good and kind as the Rosses, how could everything be bad? Surely there must be some good left in their future.

Before they left the Ross home, the Indian family named the date of departure. Jim and Sim would each take a boat to help carry the Lightfoot's belongings to St. George. On their way, they would stop by the Ross place to say their final goodbyes to Aggie, Min, and Queenie.

When the day of departure arrived, everything went as planned. When Joe and his family stopped by the Ross place, Aggie and Min supplied them with foods that would not perish as they traveled southward. When they were finally ready to pull away from the landing, there wasn't a dry eye among the women. Pete and Queenie hugged each other and cried uncontrollably. They did not know if they would ever see each other again.

"Goodbye, my little sister Queenie," said Pete. "You are my only sister now. I will always love you, just as I loved Dawn."

"You'll always be my big brother, Pete. Please come back to see us some day," said Queenie, as her tears choked away any further words.

When the boats pulled away, Queenie ran to her room and sobbed. Min respected her privacy and left her alone. She knew that Queenie was crying as much for Dawn as she was for Pete. How Min wished that Queenie had other children close by to play with! After some time, she went to Queenie's room to console her.

"Queenie, your Grandma and I want to go and try to catch a few fish for supper. Don't you want to go, too?" asked Min.

Queenie dried her eyes and answered in the affirmative. "But Ma," she cried, "what will I do now? Dawn is gone, and now Pete is gone, too. Who will I play with, or go fishin' with, or share my animals with?"

"I don't rightly know, Honey, but we'll think of something. Your Pa will just have to take you huntin' and fishin' more often, and he'll probably take you over to Traders Hill real soon. You need to go and check on Mr. Harry. I know he misses you when you don't go so often," answered Min, hugging her little golden-haired girl.

Queenie and her mother did go fishing for a little while, but any attempts by Min and Aggie to cheer Queenie were unsuccessful. Min thought to herself how relieved she would be when Sim returned. He would know what to say to Queenie to get her mind off the two friends that she would have to learn to live without.

In the days that followed, Sim did pay extra attention to his daughter. He insisted that Queenie accompany him on alligator hunts, fishing trips, and trips to Traders Hill. He even took her down to St. George with the hope that Sam would be back with news of Little Joe. Unfortunately, Sam had not returned, and Sim tried to hide his disappointment.

As Sim paddled their boat across the big lake, Queenie asked, "Do you think Pete will ever come back to see us, Pa?"

"I doubt it, Queenie. They're goin' to a place that's very far away. They'll be livin' amongst their own people and tryin' to build up a good life for themselves. They'll be livin' on a reservation where the government can't take their land away from them. Pete will be expected to marry an Indian girl and have children to carry on his people's heritage."

"I guess I was wrong, but I thought that maybe me and Pete might get married some day. I just won't ever get married now," answered Queenie.

"Oh, Queenie, you're too young to think of such things," said Sim. "Anyway, you'll need to marry somebody of your own race someday."

"Well, when Dawn married Sam, that's what made me think it's all right for me to marry an Indian. But I guess I don't need to ever get married anyway."

"Not for a long time, Honey, a very long time."

"I guess you're right, Pa." With that, the subject seemed closed. They poled their way among the water lilies over the brown swamp water toward home.

Sim and Mr. Jim had agreed to take care of the stills until Sam could get someone else to run them. They even let Queenie accompany them to the stills a few times. Aggie and Min were not sure that was a good idea, but they said nothing. If these trips to the stills helped Queenie come out of her sadness, they would allow her to go. They did worry about the fact that more renegades had recently been venturing into the swamp. If these people found an unattended still, they often took over the enterprise and claimed it for their own. So far, there had not been any trouble, but Min was anxious for Sam to return and get someone else to run the stills.

Sam finally returned to St. George and managed to get a young black man, Bo Clark, and his wife, Mattie, to agree to take over the brewing of the spirits. Sam got a fresh load of supplies, and he and the young couple headed for the swamp. He stopped by the Ross place so they could meet his new friends and Jim and Sim would know that they were relieved of their duties at the stills.

The Ross family was very glad to see Sam back home and to learn that Little Joe was in good hands. The Clarks proved to be good people, and Sim assured Sam that his family would do all they could to help them get adjusted to life in the south swamp. Because some of the Lightfoot family's camp was still intact, the young couple could stay there for awhile, but they would soon need a sturdier dwelling. Sim and Jim promised to assist them with the construction of a new cabin.

Bo had known his wife since they were children, but Mattie had only recently reached the age when her family would give their consent for her to marry. Sam was a little surprised that they agreed to move into the swamp to run the stills. The money he offered Bo, however, was too good to turn down. Both of Bo's and Mattie's families still lived in St. George, and the couple realized that they could go visit their people whenever they wanted. With the high wages

Sam had promised to pay them, they would soon have enough money to return to St. George and build their own house there. Bo could then work in the sawmill or for a logging company. For the present, however, Bo and Mattie planned to do the best they could to keep the stills going.

Sam promised to come back to the Ross home for a visit soon. He then left to take Bo and Mattie to the stills and help them get settled in their new environment. Before he left, Sim and Mr. Jim promised to go over the following day to help Bo get started with the stills and help him make plans for a new dwelling.

Sim told Bo that he must learn the swamp holler, as it was necessary to warn anyone that company was approaching. He assured Bo that any time he or his family came out to the stills, they would give fair warning of their arrival. He asked Bo and Mattie to do the same when they approached the Ross place. Running stills was a rather dangerous business, and Sim wanted these new neighbors to be safe as well as successful. Anyone new in the swamps had much to learn, and he vowed to teach them as much as possible.

Everyone spent the following days helping the Clarks get settled. Jim and Sim even allowed Queenie to help with the construction of the cabin. She was growing fast and was learning to handle tools skillfully. Bo was a big, strong man accustomed to hard work, but Mattie was only familiar with housework. However, when she saw Queenie wielding a hammer, she refused to be outdone by this little swamp girl, so she joined in the construction. Mattie took a special liking to Queenie, and a quick friendship developed between them. At lunchtime during their first day of work, Mattie asked Queenie to help her prepare the midday meal. This pleased Queenie, and she proved to be as good in the kitchen as she was with a hammer and nails.

When the stills were taken care of and the cabin was finished, it was time for the Rosses to head back home. Queenie knew she would miss her new friends. "You be sure and come over to our place soon," she said as she climbed into her family's boat.

Jim and Sim added their invitation to Queenie's, and the Clarks knew they were not alone in the swamp. Sim was relieved that

Queenie had made friends with Mattie Clark and her husband. Sim hoped that these new friends would keep Queenie's mind off the loss of the Lightfoot family.

Bo was a skillful hunter and realized quickly that the stills would not take all of his time. He decided to hunt for alligators because he knew the sale of the hides would bring in extra money. He would not leave Mattie alone while he hunted, however, so he carried her over to the Ross place anytime that he, Jim, and Sim went hunting. Aggie and Min looked forward to Mattie's visits, as did Queenie. Mattie was proficient at knitting and crocheting, and she always brought her supplies over so that she could teach these skills to the three Ross women. Aggie and Min in their turn shared their expertise as dressmakers, and so the women spent many days on the front porch of the Ross home knitting, sewing, and crocheting. As the soft breezes whispered through the low-hanging moss in the trees, the women's needles clicked in a steady rhythm. Mattie found a contentment with her new friends that she soon realized was a peace that only swamp people could know.

Chapter Eleven

☾

By 1880, when she was fourteen years old, Queenie had become quite a hunter and could catch more fish than anyone in her family. She had also become a good helper around the house, especially since Aggie had become rather feeble and Queenie's mother needed assistance with some of the household chores. There was always cooking and gardening to be done, and the chickens required much attention. Sim did the milking, but after that, the churning needed to be done. After harvest, when the vegetables were in abundance, there was lots of canning to do, and when the berries were ripe, the ladies of the house were busy making jams and jellies.

Even though Aggie spent much of her time in bed, she was still able to help with some of the cooking, and she could go to church each month when they held a meeting in Moniac. The Rosses still looked forward to seeing Min's family on these Sundays, but many new settlers had moved into the area, and church Sundays provided good opportunities to get acquainted with these new people.

One warm afternoon when Min was working in the garden, Queenie decided to go inside and talk to her grandmother for a while. When she walked into the room, Aggie looked at her in a peculiar manner. "Ma?" asked Aggie. "Is that you, Ma?"

"You must be dreamin', Grandma. It's me, Queenie. Get yourself awake, and let's talk a while."

"You are funnin' me, Ma," replied Aggie. "I've been just lying here thinkin' how I must have hurt you when I run away with Jim so long ago. But, Ma, you did understand, I know. I've missed all of you through the years, and I thought that some day I'd get back to see you, but I don't think I can now. You see, I've got old, Ma. I don't feel much like traveling now. It's too far to Carolina for these old bones to go now. Me and Jim, we've been happy, but sometimes I get so lonesome, Ma. I know you understand."

"Grandma, please wake up. You ain't talkin' to your Ma. You're just dreamin' that your Ma is here. Your Ma is dead by now, I know. You see, she'd be a hundred years old now, if she was alive. Just wake up, and let's talk to each other."

Queenie was beginning to get worried. Her grandmother seemed to be wide awake, but what she was saying did not make sense. Queenie decided to call her mother in from the garden. She went to the door and called, "Ma, come in the house. I think something has happened to Grandma. What she's sayin' don't make sense."

Min entered the room and immediately saw the blank expression on her mother-in-law's face. "Miss Aggie," said Min, "are you feelin' poorly? Let's get you a cool drink of water and see if you don't feel better."

Queenie ran for some cool water, but her Grandmother had dropped into a deep sleep by the time she returned. Jim and Sim were out on a hunt, so Queenie and her mother had to wait until the men returned to let them know about Aggie's condition. Aggie continued to sleep, and no amount of coaxing could awaken her.

When the men returned and discovered Aggie's condition, Sim rushed to Bo's cabin and asked him to go immediately to St. George to fetch the doctor. Bo brought Mattie to the Ross home, and she tried to help with Aggie. "She done gone in a coma, Miss Min," she said. "I know 'bout that 'cause that's how my Grandma went. At least she won't be in no pain, though."

Mr. Jim would not leave Aggie's bedside. He wanted to believe that she would wake again in a short while, but that was not to be. She died before the doctor arrived. The doctor examined Aggie and assured her family that there was nothing he could have done if he had been there. He felt sure that she had suffered a massive stroke, and there was no way she could have recovered from that.

Mr. Jim was inconsolable. "My life is ended," he said. "There's nothing to live for now. I just don't want to live without my Aggie."

While Min and Mattie prepared Aggie's body for burial, Queenie and Sim tried to help Mr. Jim. "Grandpa," began Queenie, "you know Grandma has gone to Heaven. The preacher says that some day we will all be together again in Heaven. You believe that, don't you, Grandpa?"

"Yes, Baby, I do believe that, but I want to be with her now," answered Mr. Jim. "I just can't go on livin' without her."

"We'll all help you, Pa," said Sim. "I don't see how any of us can go on without her, but somehow we'll have to."

Sim and Queenie were able to get Mr. Jim to walk down behind the house and choose a place for them to start a family cemetery. They chose a high spot of ground and roped off the area. The little plot was some distance from the house, but it was close enough to be seen from the windows. Bo had promised to dig the grave, and everyone knew he would have no trouble getting help with this sad chore.

When they returned from the cemetery site, Min and Mattie had finished dressing Aggie's body and had placed it on a bed in the front room. She looked so peaceful, and Jim sat by the bed, refusing to leave the room for several hours. Queenie went in and sat with him, and she held his rough old hand and talked to him of happy times gone by—times when Aggie was well and happy and taking care of everyone in the family.

Mr. Jim sat quietly and made no reply, but Queenie's presence was a great comfort to him. He believed that she understood the sorrow that was breaking his heart.

Soon the neighbors began to come in, and the house was quickly filled with these friends. Many spent the night, and all brought food and flowers to the bereaved family. No one gave a swamp holler when they approached the Ross home this time. Instead, the boats quietly and somberly pulled up to the landing.

Sim walked down to the landing where Bo was busy attending the friends as they arrived. "Bo, I can never thank you enough for taking over and helping us like you have. As long as I live, I'll never forget that you are a true friend to our family."

"I seen death many times when I was a boy back in the plantation days," answered Bo. "But I can see that this is the first death you all has had in your family. I'll help all I can, and make it as easy for you as possible."

Bo's kindness was too much, and Sim began to cry. Bo put his big arm around his friend as they walked up toward the house.

Sam and some friends from St. George arrived, and Sam told Sim that he had sent word to Henry Cooper, who could not get there in time for the funeral the following day. He knew, however, that the Ross family would want their friend in St. Marys to know about this sad event.

Bo and Sam constructed the casket, and Min and Mattie lined the homemade burial box with a soft white cloth. Aggie's body was placed in the casket where she would rest. The preacher from the Moniac church was there to direct the funeral, and Aggie was buried in the new family cemetery. The service took place in the early afternoon, and soon after, all their friends had returned to their homes. Bo and Mattie, however, insisted on remaining until dark. They knew there was a meal to prepare and beds to get back in order after use by the overnight guests. Meanwhile, they insisted that everyone else just sit on the porch while they prepared supper and straightened the house. The Rosses were grateful for their help, and Bo and Mattie were glad that they could repay their friends for some of the kindness that had been shown to them.

When Mattie went out to the porch to ask if she could get anything for anyone, she was startled to find that they were all gone.

They had all gone back down to the little gravesite to be with Aggie again and to straighten the many flower arrangements that had been placed there.

Henry came up to see his friends within a few days. They made plans to meet in Traders Hill at a later date, when Henry would have some papers for them to sign. He had obtained two more small tracts of land for Sim and his family, and he also suggested that, while they were in Traders Hill, they should go ahead and order a tombstone for Aggie's grave. Sim told him that Mr. Jim might not be able to come with him, but that he would be there on the appointed date.

As it turned out, Jim did not feel up to going to Traders Hill with his son, but Queenie was glad to go along. She could now drive the ox cart as well as anyone in the family, so she was a great help to Sim on the journey. They spent the day with Harry at his house and transacted their business there. Harry was as busy as always, making furniture and carving figures of all kinds. His reputation had grown even more since so many new people were moving into southeast Georgia.

Henry told them that many of these new people were from other parts of the country. Some were even former Yankee soldiers who had become familiar with the South while they served in the Federal army. New settlements were springing up everywhere, but most of the new settlers were moving into St. Marys and the other coastal areas. They had learned about the recreation that could be found in the swamp, so more people than ever were venturing into the area to hunt and fish.

Sim told Henry that some of these hunters and fishermen were trespassing on Ross property, but so far Sim had seen no reason to restrict their activities. In fact, Sim thought it was best for some of the abundance of animals to be cleared out. He was making enough money from timber in the lower part of the swamp that he did not need to make money from hunting the alligators or other animals. As long as they did not bother the Ross trees and were careful about fire, they were welcome.

Sim also told Henry that their neighbors in the swamp still did not know that the Ross family owned most of the south swamp, and Sim made it plain that they wanted to keep it that way. If people realized that the Rosses had so much land and money, they would probably no longer be accepted by their neighbors. To Sim and his family, friends were more valuable than money, and they did not want to do anything to jeopardize any of these relationships.

They told Harry about Aggie's death, and he cried when he heard the news. He remembered how good Aggie had been to him after the terrible snake bite. He insisted that Henry take him out to the Ross place very soon so he could visit Mr. Jim and the rest of the family, and Henry promised to do so.

Sim ordered the grave marker and made plans to return to Traders Hill when it arrived. Henry made plans to meet him again soon, and they departed for their respective homes.

Queenie enjoyed her visit with Mr. Henry and Mr. Harry and loaded the cart with several carved pieces and a very pretty little cabinet. The drawers fit perfectly, and the wood had been polished to a beautiful sheen.

"I miss having Grandpa with us today, but it has still been a good day," said Queenie. "We did get to see Mr. Henry and Mr. Harry. They're such good friends, ain't they, Pa?"

"Yes, they are, Queenie. I miss Pa, too," said Sim, "but I'm beginnin' to wonder if he'll ever want to go anywhere again. He's takin' Ma's death harder than anybody I ever saw. I wish I knew what to do to help him, but I'm afraid that he's makin' himself sick. He won't eat right, and he just sits and stares or stays down at Ma's little gravesite."

"I'll never tell him what Grandma said just before she died, Pa. She thought she was talking to her Ma, you know, but what was so sad was that she said she had missed her family through the years and that she had hoped to get back to see her Ma some day. She said that her and Grandpa had been happy but sometimes she had been lonesome. I think Grandpa would feel so bad if he knew she said that."

"I guess we should have tried to take her back for a visit once we had the money. I thought about it, but I knew her Ma would be dead by this time, and it would've just made her sad to go back. I guess they just didn't have the money for the trip when they were younger."

"Sometimes life is hard, ain't it, Pa?"

"That's right, Honey, but we just have to do the best we can and go on with our lives."

When Sim and Queenie returned from their trip to Traders Hill, Min had supper ready, and she was sitting on the porch waiting for them. Jim was slowly walking up from the little graveyard, and tears were streaming down his face. Queenie ran up to him and took hold of his hand. "Come on in, Grandpa, and let me show you the pretty things Mr. Harry made for me. He's comin' out to see us soon. He 'specially wants to visit with you."

Mr. Jim followed her into the house and looked at her new gifts, but his mind seemed to be somewhere else. She led him in to supper, but he ate very little. He soon excused himself and went to sit on the front porch. His family was worried about him, but Sim said he thought his Pa would soon be back to himself.

Sim went out of his way to plan fishing trips with his father. He took him on hunting trips, and he even took him over to St. George, hoping a visit with Sam would cheer him up. Jim went along to please Sim, but he showed very little interest in anything Sim planned. Sim still felt that his father would soon come out of his deep gloom, but Jim continued to grieve for Aggie.

Within six months, Mr. Jim was dead. He had lost too much weight, and when winter set in, he took a bad cold that grew into pneumonia. He was not able to overcome this illness and passed away quickly and peacefully. Their friends came as they had when Aggie died, and Bo and Mattie came once again to help their friends. The preacher from the Moniac church conducted the funeral, and Mr. Jim was laid to rest beside his beloved Aggie.

Within a short time, Sim had another marker, much like the one he had purchased for Aggie's grave, placed at Jim's grave. They were together now—two people who had loved each other enough to defy her entire family and isolate themselves where they could build the kind of life they wanted together. Sim could not help thinking of what Queenie had told him about Aggie's last words. Sim knelt by the two markers and shed tears for what might have been. He wept because Aggie was with her mother at last, and she had her beloved Jim with her once again. As he knelt at their graves, he asked God to watch over the two new angels who had come to him from their home in the south Georgia swamps.

Chapter Twelve

☾

The 1880s brought about quite a few changes in the lives of the Ross family. As Queenie grew into young adulthood, she became a typical swamper. She fished, hunted, went to and from Traders Hill with her father, and helped her mother with the housework. She also became a lead singer at church and made many friends whom she enjoyed seeing there each month. Min's brothers continued to keep busy at the sawmill, so Queenie did not see them very often. She did, however, enjoy seeing Min's parents and sisters regularly. They still lived in their old home near the Suwannee River.

Sim and Min had assumed that Queenie would take an interest in at least one of the young men she saw at church. This, however, did not happen. She enjoyed their friendship as she did the friendship of the girls, but that was all. She attended the social gatherings at church—the "sings" and the dinners—but she showed no special interest in the boys. Several had gotten up enough nerve to ask to "come calling," but Queenie always put them off by telling them she had work to do at home and did not have time to receive visitors. Min worried about Queenie's apparent lack of interest in dating, but Sim always said that sooner or later, Queenie's interests would change.

"Some day we won't be around to look after her, Sim," said Min. "I hope we'll see her married and settled down before then."

"I've thought about that too, Min. But there's plenty of time for that. We'll just be patient and see what happens," answered Sim. "In the meantime, we'll do all we can to teach her to take care of herself. She's pretty independent, as you know. One thing for sure, at least she won't ever have to worry about money."

In recent months, Sam Smith had come to visit them, and he finally told them about his past. The man who had threatened his life had recently died, so Sam could finally use his real name. When he introduced himself as Ben LaFlour, Min and Sim were surprised. But they were pleased that he could now put that part of his past behind him. He told them that he had wanted his son, Joe, to come and live with him. The boy, however, had become so attached to his father's family that he did not want to leave them. Although disappointed, Ben accepted his son's decision and gave his family ample money to take care of the child. He was a wealthy man now, since he had made so much money from a logging business he owned and from the stills that Bo and Mattie operated for him.

Another change in Ben's life was that he had married a very nice lady from St. George, named Mae. Ben and his new wife visited the Ross home often, and both families became close friends. When Ben came down to the stills or to hunt and fish, Mae accompanied him and spent time with Min. Since Mae's mother was no longer living, Min became like a mother to her. When Mae's children came along, Min gave her advice about motherhood.

As the years passed, Bo and Mattie expanded their family as well. Bo was doing so well with the stills that when the children came along, he and Mattie decided to remain in the swamp and simply build onto their cabin. They often visited their families in St. George, but the south swamp became their home. They spent much of their time at the Ross home, and Queenie became the idol of the children. Min had done a good job of teaching Queenie to read, write, and do her figuring, so Queenie decided to pass this knowledge on to the

Clark children. She spent many days on the front porch teaching the little black children to read, write, and work with figures.

There were times when Queenie thought about the fact that her parents were getting older, and she wondered what would happen to her in the years to come. She remembered how suddenly her grandmother had died and how quickly her grandfather had followed. She did not dwell on these things, but one day she did bring up the subject to Sim when they were quietly fishing out on the big lake. "Pa," she began, "I sometimes wonder what I'll be doin' when I get old like Grandma and Grandpa were. If I'm left alone in the swamp, I wonder if I'll be able to make enough money to keep goin'. I know we can sell some of the trees from time to time, but I'm wonderin' if they'll last as long as I'll need a little money to buy what I need."

Sim suddenly realized that he had not been open enough with his daughter, who was now obviously old enough to think about her future. This was the time to let her know the truth about their finances. "Perhaps I should have told you long ago, Queenie," he said, "but somehow I didn't realize how fast you were growin' up. I don't want folks to know it, but we are rich, Queenie. We not only own most of the south swamp now, but we have thousands of dollars in Henry's bank at St. Marys."

"I don't understand, Pa. I thought we just owned a few trees to sell to the loggers and sawmillers."

"I guess it's time for me to tell you the whole story, Queenie," answered Sim. "Bear in mind, though, that nobody ever knew about this but my Ma and Pa, your mother, Henry Cooper, and me. It's a long story. Do you think you can hold out to listen for an hour or so?"

"Of course I can, Pa. But what on earth could take that long to tell about? You've got me curious now," she said. "Go ahead, Pa. I've got nothin' else to do but listen."

So Sim at last told his daughter the whole story of the Confederate gold, how he and Jim had hidden it, and finally how Henry Cooper had traded it for modern currency. Sim explained how Henry had helped him to buy up land as it came on the market. "You see, Queenie, most folks thought this swamp land was worthless because so much of it was under water. But Pa realized its value, and so did Henry. We actually own thousands of acres of the south swamp and, as I told you, we have thousands of dollars from the sale of timber. And we're sellin' more all the time.

"Now, I want you to understand what I told you about the gold. I didn't steal it. I've never stolen anything. I would've returned it to the outfit if I'd known where to find 'em. I simply did the only thing I could think of to keep it out of Federal hands, and maybe keep myself out of prison."

"Oh, Pa, you were so smart to do that! I'm so proud of you. Ma has told me all about what a brave soldier you were and how she prayed for you to come back from the war. I'm wondering, though, Pa, why are we pretending to be just poor swampers? I don't think the Yankee soldiers would worry about Confederate gold after all this time."

"I don't think they would, either, but if we started throwin' money around, we'd lose our friends here in the swamp. Most folks around here are poor. There are some well-off folks in the north swamp, up around Suwannee and around Black Hammock, and around Billy's Island and Billy's Lake and Floyd's Island. But we had the advantage to get more land here in the south swamp because there's fewer people down here. Up around Black Hammock I hear there's some very rich timber land, but it's been bought up by now. One family owns most of that area, and I'm sure they're very wealthy. But I run into some of these folks from time to time at Traders Hill, and you would never know they were well-off. Swampers don't show off what they have. They just live and let live, as the sayin' goes. Most of the people that I see at Traders Hill belong to the Sardis Church, and I understand they have a big congregation there. Maybe sometime we'll go up to one of their sings."

"That would be fun, Pa," answered Queenie. "We could add our good singin' to theirs. I'm glad you told me all of this, Pa. I do see, too, why you want to keep quiet about what we have."

"And there's one more thing, Queenie. If you and your Ma ever want to move to one of the towns on the outside, just let me know, and we'll do it."

"Oh, no, Pa, I don't think we could ever be happy out among all those people. Of course, I'm willin' to do anything you and Ma want to do, but this is where I'm happiest. This is our land, and these are our trees and our animals and birds. I hope we can always stay where we are."

"Well, I guess we'd better get on home. Your Ma will be worryin' 'bout us 'cause we've been gone so long. I don't have a single fish on my line, though, and she wanted fresh fish for supper."

"Don't worry, Pa," laughed Queenie. "I've got a good string of perch in the back of the boat. They're hanging over the side to keep fresh. Let's get home and start cookin'."

Min already had the oil in the washpot ready for the fresh perch. She'd made up the hushpuppies and had them ready to cook, and she dumped them into the pot while Sim and Queenie cleaned the fish.

After a good meal, the little family sat on the front porch until dark. The peace and quiet of the swamp was broken only by an owl in the distance and the chirping of birds high in the cypress trees.

Sim told Min of his and Queenie's conversation, and he told her that he had offered to move them to the outside any time they wished. But Queenie, he told her, had said that she preferred to remain in the swamp.

Min agreed that it was time that Queenie knew this family secret. She was glad that Sim had told their daughter the whole story.

"Now, Pa," asked Queenie, "how could any place on the outside ever be as quiet and peaceful as this?"

"You're right, Honey," answered Sim, and Min nodded in complete agreement. "There's no other place like it."

Talking about those Confederate days made Sim want to go down to the barn and check on his old horse, Bob. No longer did any of them try to ride Bob. He was getting too old, and he now received the best of care from the whole family. Sim still held a special place in his heart for this old friend who had brought him home from the war.

"Well, Bob," Sim said softly when he entered the barn, "I've told our little girl our secret. She had to know about it sometime. That's been a long time ago, Bob, but you've been with us through all these years, and you know all of our secrets. It's worked out all right, hasn't it? I know you miss Ma and Pa. They were proud of you, Bob, 'cause you brought me back home after all them hard years of war. I hope you've been happy down in these swamps. I just wanted to check on you to see that you're all right. Now, you get a good night's rest." He lovingly patted the old horse and told him good night.

Sim walked back up to the porch where Min and Queenie were quietly singing one of their favorite tunes. Sim joined his voice with theirs, and they in turn were joined by the birds in the nearby trees and an owl in the distance. All the voices were in harmony.

When the song was finished, Sim decided that it was bedtime for the Ross family, and time to let the swamp animals rest, too. As they prepared to enter the house, they could see a full moon peeping through the branches of the cypress trees.

"See, Pa," said Queenie, as she pointed toward the heavens, "there ain't nothing on earth prettier than that."

"You're right, Honey," Sim replied, placing one arm around his wife and the other around his daughter. Together they went inside the snug, simple house for a peaceful night's rest.

Chapter Thirteen

☾

By 1900, additional small towns had grown up all around the swamp. Most of these towns were only sawmill camp towns, and as the timber in the area was felled, the sawmillers usually moved on to the next campsite. The short railroad lines over near the coast brought in more settlers as jobs became available in the mills and on the farms and in the booming coastal fishing industry.

All of these developments meant only minor changes for the swampers. They continued to produce an abundance of farm products that could be sold in the sawmill camps. Chickens, eggs, and pork sold well, as did fresh fruit and vegetables. The swampers enjoyed taking their products to market, and many swamp people prospered during the l900s. Some even moved out to the small surrounding settlements.

The Ross family, the Clark family, and Min's family, however, remained at their old homesteads. Even so, they began to feel less isolated as the railroad lines came down from the coastal towns. The real excitement, however, was the big railroad that was creeping its way up from Jacksonville. It would go through St. George, Moniac, Fargo, and on to Valdosta, and Sim found himself making more and more trips to St. George to check with Ben LaFlour concerning the progress of the railroad. Ben was becoming very wealthy from his logging business, which supplied crossties for the railroad construction. Sim, in turn, was making money because he sold acre after acre of cypress trees to Ben's company. He was also selling pine trees to the lumber camps for the construction of houses and for raw timber.

As the railroad crawled up through north Florida and south Georgia, Sim made many trips to keep up with the construction, and Queenie insisted on accompanying him on these excursions. Min even came along from time to time.

Ben had built a nice house in St. George for his wife, Mae, and their children, Jed and Mary. The children were receiving a fairly good education from the school that had been organized in St. George. By 1900, Jed was sixteen years old, and Mary was fourteen. They enjoyed their visits to the Ross home, and very seldom was their father able to go to the south swamp without one or both of them tagging along.

When Sim saw the nice house Ben was building, he was inspired to make some improvements on his own home. The house on Ross Island was comfortable, so he saw no need to put too much effort into changing the place. He did hang new screens on the windows and doors to try to keep out the mosquitoes that were a constant nuisance, and he made a few other minor improvements as well.

Bo and Mattie were prospering, too. Sim had offered them the use of any of the Ross land they needed down around their place to grow fresh produce to sell to the lumber camps. So when Bo carried a load of spirits to St. George, he also carried fresh vegetables, chickens, eggs, and fresh meat. He bought a large new boat for this purpose, and he and Mattie felt very grand as they paddled and poled their fine boat to and from the outside.

The Clark children, Bobo and Matilda, who was called Tilda, were developing into healthy swamp children. As they matured, Queenie continued to teach them as much as she could. They were both smart, and they wanted to learn. They talked often about the time when they would leave the swamp. Queenie knew that some day they would indeed be leaving, so she hoped to do as much as she could to help prepare them for the outside. Bo and Mattie, however, had no plans to move back to the outside. They were making more money now than they could hope to make outside the swamp.

During the 1900s, Sim and his family began to venture a little more to the outside. Sim talked with swampers from the extreme eastern part of the swamp when he made his trips to Traders Hill. They insisted that Sim and his family attend church there when they could and take part in their songfests. This proved to be a source of pleasure to the Ross family, and Sim and Min were especially glad that Queenie could associate with other young people.

The families who lived in the central and north swamp did most of their trading at the town of Waycross and at some of the small towns just north of the swamp. Some of these people did attend the Sardis Church and shop at Traders Hill from time to time, so Sim and his family became acquainted with them, too.

In the early 1900s, the Rosses' faithful horse, Bob, died. His death was particularly hard on Sim because it brought back so many memories of the war years. Much time had passed since Sim had ridden his beautiful Confederate horse down to the south swamp, but memories of the war still lingered in Sim's mind. In fact, Sim knew now that those memories would never leave him. They had faded somewhat as time passed, but he never would be able to completely forget those four long years of suffering and death.

When Sim was away hunting one day, Min called Queenie back to a storage room and showed her Sim's Confederate uniform and a Confederate flag. "Now, Queenie," she said, "I'm goin' to do something I promised Miss Aggie I'd do for her. By all laws of nature, you should outlive both your Pa and me. Miss Aggie asked me to promise her, in case Sim dies before I do, that I'd bury him in his old uniform and drape this flag over his coffin. If he outlives me, then I'm askin' you to carry out Miss Aggie's wishes. We've taken care of the uniform and the flag, and if you outlive me, I'll depend on you to take care of it and do as Miss Aggie wished. Now, I'm not telling you this to make you sad, 'cause I hope we'll be around a long time. It does relieve my mind, though, to tell you this," concluded Min.

"I promise to do as you say, Ma," said Queenie. "I know that's how Pa would want it to be. I know you are proud that Pa was a brave soldier, and so am I."

None of the new acquaintances that Queenie made at Sardis Church or the songfests triggered any romance. She had made many new friends, both girls and boys, but none of the boys ever became more than just friends. Queenie still preferred the company of her parents, the Clark family, and Ben LaFlour's family. She saw no need to ever leave her parents. This was where she was happy and where she belonged.

With the new influx of outsiders came some very rough people. The Rosses did not have any trouble, but Sim cautioned Min and Queenie to be more careful. Keeping a shotgun handy was now necessary, because from time to time, strangers approached the Ross place without giving the swamp holler. They were informed that people did not enter the Ross run without giving the holler that signaled their approach, and a shotgun pointed at such a person emphasized this caution.

Bo, however, began to have quite a bit of trouble defending the stills. Several times he had been forced to fire his gun. He had not shot anyone, but the gunfire drove off those who would have caused trouble. The situation was such that he would not leave Mattie and the children alone, and he could never be away from the stills when there was a good amount of spirits on hand. After all, the stills did not belong to him—they belonged to Ben LaFlour. Bo would do his best to defend Ben's property.

Ben knew that sooner or later he would be forced to give up the making of spirits. Bo was doing so well, though, that Ben hated to deprive him of his good-paying enterprise. The Clark family loved their home in the south swamp and dreaded the day when they would have to return to the outside.

The chief excitement continued to be the big Southern Railroad that reached St. George and crawled on toward Valdosta. A nice depot was built in each town, and houses for the railroad workers were nice as well. The Ross family and the other swampers made a point to be in these towns when the train was due to arrive. Sim had seen railroads and trains during the war when he was moving from place to place, but never did he dream that a railroad would be built such a short distance from the Ross place. Lumber as well as other products could now be shipped by rail, and people could travel from town to town and even down to Jacksonville and other Florida towns. By 1898, the railroad had reached Valdosta, and as a result, this town, as well as other connecting towns, began to grow rapidly.

In 1898, however, a new situation began to worry Sim. Newspapers were now being delivered into the towns by train, so even the swamp people were able to keep up with the news of the day. More often, Sim was reading about the situation down in Cuba. There were all kinds of reports of mistreatment of the Cubans by the Spanish. The United States government had warned Spain about the trouble there, but the situation did not seem to improve. War with Spain seemed almost imminent.

Sim knew what war meant. He knew that he was now too old to be personally involved in a war with Spain, but any mention of war worried him. He thought of the young men he knew who might be sent to such a war and what might happen to them.

The United States had sent the Battleship Maine to the harbor of Havana, Cuba, and it was destroyed. War with Spain was declared, and the cry all over the country was, "Remember the Maine!" Sim read of all the excitement and learned that many of the leaders of the Civil War were taking part in preparations for this war. Even though these men were professional soldiers, Sim wondered how they could go into battle again after all they had experienced in the Civil War. One thing was certain, even if he were still a young man, he could never go through that again.

The shock of the whole situation came to him when he heard a familiar holler one day soon after war was declared. Ben LaFlour pulled up to the landing with a very worried expression on his face. Sim met him down at the dock and realized immediately that something was wrong.

"I hope you are not busy, Sim. I just had to come and talk with you," said Ben. He held a letter, which he now handed to Sim. It was from his sister and told the news of Little Joe.

"My boy, Joe, has gone to join the army that's goin' to Cuba, Sim. I don't want him down there. I don't want him to be a coward, but he's too young to know what he's doin'. Is there anything I can do to stop him? What can I do?"

"I can't rightly think of anything you can do, Ben. He is of age now to join the army, and at his age, a person can get caught up in the excitement of war. Try not to worry. The United States Army is very powerful, and that war should be over soon."

"In the letter, my sister, Sari, says that Joe is in training in Tampa, Florida now. He hopes to sail to Cuba soon. I feel so guilty about the whole thing, Sim. If he had been livin' with me, maybe I could have talked him out of it."

"I doubt if you could have stopped him, Ben," said Sim. "When a young person makes up his mind on somethin' like that, it's hard to stop him."

"I know you're probably right," sighed Ben. "Sari says in the letter that Joe didn't ask anybody about goin'. He just came in, picked up his belongings, said his goodbyes, and left."

Sim knew that Sam's father had passed away, and only his mother, his Uncle Jed, and his sister, Sari, were still at home. His other sisters were married and living elsewhere. Sim knew how worried these people must be after watching Joe leave for a war in a foreign country. He could certainly sympathize with them, as well as for Ben, because he remembered how his parents had worried about him when he was in the army.

"You must not feel guilty about this, Ben," he said. "I know how hard you tried to get Joe to come and live with you. Now, let's just all hope and pray that Joe gets back safe and sound. That's really all we can do at this point."

"I know you're right, Sim. Besides the fighting, though, I've been readin' about all the diseases down there. The Yellow Fever just kills people off in droves. I know they'll have army doctors there, so we'll just have to hope and pray for the best. I do feel better since I talked to you, Sim. I'll keep you posted about my boy's well-bein'. I have to go over and check on Bo and his family, but I'll be seein' you soon."

Sim stood for a long time watching his friend pole his way down the run. How he hoped that Joe would get back alive. He stood there remembering Dawn and the baby she had brought into the world. What a long time ago that had been, and how many changes had taken place among the swamp families since that time. He was glad that the Lightfoot family did not know about Joe's planning to fight in a foreign country, a country where disease was prevalent and posed an added threat to Joe's life.

Sim walked slowly back up to the house. He dreaded to tell this news to Min and Queenie. Ben LaFlour's family was very close to them, and even though Joe had never been back to St. George since he left as an infant, they had kept up with him through the years. As Sim walked back toward the house, he breathed a prayer for the safety of Little Joe as he faced the dangers of war in a foreign country.

Chapter Fourteen

☾

The war in Cuba lasted only three months, but many Americans died in battle or of disease, particularly yellow fever. Little Joe was killed at the Battle of Kettle Hill. His family received word from his commanding officer that he had been a brave soldier and had died with honor.

When Ben received word of his son's death, he went to see Sim to pour out his grief. Somehow he knew that Sim would understand. He had faced the hardships of battle so many years ago and would fully understand the dangers that were faced in combat.

Sim did understand, and he grieved with his friend. The entire Ross family grieved as well, since Joe was Dawn's child. They could all remember the bittersweet day when Little Joe was born. How they wished they could have seen Joe from time to time as he was growing up. Now they would never get to know this young man whom Ben described as very handsome and loving.

Ben's wife, Mae, grieved over Joe's death as well. Even though he had never come to live with them, she had grown to love him. She had visited Ben's family near the town of Mayday and had become acquainted with Joe there.

After some months had passed, Ben shared some more shocking news for the Ross family. He had received a letter from his sister, Sari, saying that Joe was the father of an infant son. Evidently Joe had not known he had a child on the way when he left for Cuba. The child's mother had died at childbirth, and her parents were very poor, so the child's grandmother had requested that Ben's sister and his uncle rear the baby. They agreed to do so, and they named him Joseph William LaFlour. Everyone called him "Will."

Ben had gone immediately to see his grandson and offered to rear the child himself. His sister and uncle, however, had become attached to the baby and requested that Ben allow them to raise him. Ben agreed, even though he and Mae were disappointed. Ben consoled himself, however, by looking to the future when Will would be old enough to visit his grandparents. He was a beautiful child, and Ben had no doubt that he would be a handsome man some day.

Travel to Ben's parents' homeplace outside of Mayday was much easier now that the train passed through the town. Ben and his family made this trip often and enjoyed seeing little Will grow into a strong, healthy child. He did not have any Indian features but was instead a blond child who favored his mother, Maizie, and her family. He proved to be a great blessing to the LaFlour family as they tried to recover from the loss of Joe.

During the first decade of the 1900s, the timber industry continued to bring in more settlers. Most of these new people lived on the outside, but quite a few of them seemed to think that the animals in the swamp were theirs for the taking. Bo continued to run Ben's stills, but other people had begun to move into the swamps and set up stills of their own. Some of these were on Ross land, but they were so isolated that Sim decided not to run them out of the swamp unless they caused trouble. He realized that they probably did not know that they were on private property. As long as they did not interfere with Ben's operation, Ben and Sim decided not to make an issue of these infringements. Ben and Bo could sell whatever spirits Bo produced. This influx of questionable characters, however, was beginning to bring a bad reputation to the south swamp. The sawmills were now hiring many undesirable people, and since so many of them were now venturing into the swamp, many of the old-time swampers were on the alert for trouble.

One incident occurred in 1904 that brought a bad name to the south swamp that was impossible to completely overcome. Several well-to-do outsiders had moved down from other areas of the state to set up sawmilling plants. These were flourishing, and the owners were not always careful about the type of people they hired. One such mill owner had the bright idea to use the new railroad to take his workers, both black and white, on a one-day holiday to St. Augustine, Florida.

All went well the first part of the day, but when they met to board the train after a long day in the sun—a day of eating and heavy drinking—those in charge could see that trouble was brewing between the white men and the black men. There were tauntings and slurs between the two groups, and the trouble increased as the train sped north. Soon the situation became violent, and the train stopped in St. George just long enough for the conductor to wire ahead for help when the train reached Baxter.

Upon their arrival at the Baxter station, many passengers jumped off the train before it even stopped. The women and children were hustled to safety, but the unrest and threats of violence persisted. Finally, several days later, the Florida State Militia was mobilized and brought in by train. They were able to get the situation under control, arrest the chief offenders, and bring these men to trial. They were all acquitted, however, because so many people feared that a conviction would bring violent retaliation from the family members of the men who were on trial.

For some time, fear reigned in southeast Georgia, especially along the St. Marys and Suwanee River areas. Ben took his family to the Ross home and left them there until the situation quieted down. He and Sim went to Fargo and up the river to check on Min's family. They were all right, and Sim insisted that they remain alert and well armed.

Eventually the whole situation subsided, but the scars remained. Many people left the area forever, and the reputation of lawlessness in the south swamp persisted. Many large sawmill owners who could have brought wealth to the area avoided the swamp, which was considered one of the most dangerous places in the state.

St. George was not affected as much as Baxter, Moniac, and Fargo. The sawmilling did not stop, but the large operators were moving elsewhere. Mae and the children returned home and took up life as usual, and the Ross family were luckily unaffected by the "Baxter Rebellion," as it was called. The only sign of trouble was their sadness that some of their church friends from Moniac had been killed, and their sadness that their beloved south swamp was now considered a place of danger.

Slowly, the little towns south of the swamp began to rebuild their communities. The Georgia Southern and Florida Railroad kept them alive. Timber and other products were being shipped by rail, and roads were built to connect these towns. They were dirt roads, but at least they were passable. Schools were built along the edge of the south swamp, and even more were built along the north swamp. New communities, such as Folkston, were developing, and Traders Hill even began to lose some of its business and population as the new towns grew.

Sim still met Henry Cooper at Traders Hill to transact business. Harry, however, was not well, so Henry had persuaded him to move to St. Marys. This saddened Sim and Queenie, but they realized that it was the best thing for Harry. Henry kept his house near Traders Hill, but it remained vacant except when Henry used it to conduct business in town.

Ben's grandson, Will, was growing into a very dependable boy. By the time he was ten years old, he was traveling alone by train to visit his grandfather and his family. Will's aunt and uncle put him on the train in Mayday, and Ben would meet his train when it arrived in St. George. The railroad connections were making such trips an everyday occurrence.

Ben knew that the Ross family had a special interest in Dawn's grandchild, so Will's trips to St. George always included a visit to the Ross place. Ben enjoyed showing him life in the swamp, and he taught him the things that he had wanted to teach Little Joe but had never had the chance. Mae and the LaFlour children enjoyed Will's visits and looked forward to them with much anticipation.

Ben owned a fine buggy, and Will loved to ride to the nearby towns with his grandfather and his family. Sometimes Ben and Will would go alone on little trips, which pleased Will, especially when Ben let him take the reins and drive the buggy. These excursions were a great pleasure, but Will was always happy when it was time to board the train for Mayday. He missed his family, and he loved the farm and all of his friends who lived there.

Sim was always glad to see how happy Ben was when he had his grandson with him. He realized, too, that in spite of the happy family that Ben now had, he had never forgotten Dawn and would always have a special place in his heart for her and for their son, Joe.

Ben and Mae's children had grown into fine young adults, and soon Jed was old enough to join his father in the logging business. He married and established a home in St. George near his parents, and Mary married in 1908 and moved to Folkston. With their improving means of transportation, they could all visit each other from time to time quite easily.

The Ross family, however, continued to live very much as they had always lived. They still traveled chiefly by horseback when they were outside the swamp, and Queenie had her own horse and was a strong rider. Sim and Min had their own horses as well, and each of these strong animals could take them to the outside as long as they kept to the high spots on the eastern edge of the swamp. If there was a bad rainy spell, however, not even the horses could travel through the bog.

Sim was becoming less physically active as the years passed, but he still concentrated on the farming. Min did some gardening, but most of her work included the household chores. Even Queenie was beginning to show her age. She was now in her forties and was a typical swamp woman. She worked in the tobacco patch and the vegetable garden, and when she delivered produce to the camps, no one who saw her would have dreamed that this woman wearing an old-fashioned bonnet and a gingham dress was actually queen of the south swamp. How shocked they would have been to know that she and her parents had thousands and thousands of dollars in the bank at St. Marys, and that they owned many thousands of acres in the south swamp! Those who bought her produce thought they were doing her a favor. Indeed they were, because this was what Queenie enjoyed. She was happy to mingle with the people on the outside, to see what their life was like, and to make friends with them. When the trading was over, however, she and Sim were always happy to return to Min and their quiet home.

Even with the accumulated years and her exposure to the elements as she worked, Queenie was still pretty. Her hair remained golden, and her blue eyes sparkled with the inner happiness that she felt. And as she sat on the porch at the end of a day's work, Queenie often wondered what Pete now looked like. He would be in his forties as well. She wondered if he looked wrinkled and old from his life in the Florida sun. What did his wife look like? Was she pretty? How many children did they have? Did he ever think of her and her family, or had he forgotten them? There was no way to answer these questions, but it was pleasant to remember the happy times when they were children. She smiled a little as she remembered the hard time he had given her when her boat went from under her on the big lake. She still shuddered to think what would have happened to her if he had not come to her rescue and shot that terrible moccasin. He was a good friend, a very good friend. Queenie breathed a prayer for him and his family.

As she sat in the quietness of the early twilight, she heard a faint holler in the distance. She recognized it as Bo's and went inside to alert her parents that company was coming. When Bo and his family arrived, Bo said, "We just decided to come over and sit a spell, and bring you a mess of this good corn."

"Do come in and sit a while," said Sim, as he met them down at the landing.

"We have just run off some good spirits," said Bo. "If you get to feelin' poorly any time, you might need a little for medicine."

"You must have smelled the fresh cake I baked today," laughed Min. "Queenie, how about gettin' all of us a good slice of cake and some fresh milk."

Queenie followed Min's suggestion, and they spent a happy evening in good conversation and merriment. Bo had brought along his fiddle, and Sim led the group in one song after another. Bo's deep base voice was a delight to hear, and Mattie's high soprano echoed through the evening breeze. Sim, Min, Queenie, and the adult Clark children joined their voices in the melodies.

"What a pity all the folks on the outside can't hear our pretty singing," commented Mattie. "Now, let's sing some old-fashioned Negro spirituals." Bo led these songs, and all the others joined in. There was a closeness, a real love between these two families.

"I've saved the news we came to tell you till last," said Bo, as he put away his fiddle. "Mr. Ben says he's gonna close the stills soon. It's gettin' too dangerous to run 'em now. All kinds of folks is settin' up stills down in this area, and I've had to run folks off our place several times. I'm afraid for my family. We'll be movin' down to St. George, and Mr. Ben will give me work in his logging business. We'll be missin' you all, but we'll be comin' out to see you from time to time."

"We'll sure expect you to come often," said Sim.

Min and Queenie added their regret to see the Clarks moving, but all of the Rosses knew it was wise for them to do so. Running stills had certainly become a dangerous business.

"We'll bring our boats over and help you move," said Sim. "You are our good friends, and all you have to do is let us know when you're ready to pack up, and we'll be there to help."

The full moon had climbed high in the sky as all three members of the Ross family walked their friends down to the landing and sadly watched them pole their way down the run.

Chapter Fifteen

☾

As newspapers and mail became increasingly available, the swampers no longer felt so isolated. The papers and mail had to be picked up at a nearby town, but this was not as much of a problem as it had been in the past. Ben was especially thoughtful about bringing the mail and newspapers with him when he made trips to the Ross place. When Sim and his family went to the lumber camps to sell produce, they bought current newspapers and picked up any scraps of news that were passed on by the sawmill friends they encountered at the camps.

They were able to keep up with the news of the country as well as that from around the world. By 1917, Ben was beginning to be very worried about the situation in Europe. The major countries of that continent were at war. President Woodrow Wilson had promised to keep the United States out of the conflict, but many people felt that America would eventually become involved. The chief worry that Ben had was that his grandson, Will, would be called into the military. Ben's son, Jed, was old enough that he was not likely to be drafted into the army, but Will was just the right age. Ben discussed this situation with Sim.

"I can't help thinkin' what happened to his Pa down in Cuba," Ben said. "I just don't want my grandson involved in a war, especially one so for away, but I don't know what I can do about it."

"I guess there's nothing you can do, Ben," replied Sim. "Of course, we'll all pray for the boy, but when boys are young like Will is, they see the glamour of war. I can still remember how excited I was back when I volunteered for the Confederate Army. To be sure, that was a different situation. Our Southland was involved. These countries are fightin' each other, and it's not really our business."

"I just hope it will be over before our country gets involved."

"I hope so too, Ben. Even if we get into it, and Will goes into the army, he might not have to go overseas."

This was some consolation to Ben. Sim always helped him. He was older and in many ways much wiser. Ben returned home feeling somewhat relieved of his worry about Will, but he continued to grasp every bit of news he could about the situation in Europe.

Of course, the United States did get involved in the war, and in 1917, Will volunteered for the army. By this time, Will's Uncle Jed had died, and only his Aunt Sari was left behind at the homeplace. Will left with great expectations of serving his country, and there was no doubt in his mind that he was doing the right thing. This, however, did not keep the older members of his family and his friends from worrying.

Due to the war, the timber from Georgia's swamps was in large demand because huge new shipyards were in full operation up in Savannah, and the naval stores industry was developing at nearby Brunswick. Lumber was needed for housing the workers, and the sawmills were prospering. The Rosses, as well as other small farmers, sold anything they could spare to the people at the sawmill camps. As a result, the farmers increased the amount of crops that they planted. They planted as much cotton as they could handle, as well as tobacco, both of which became good moneymaking crops. Even though the Ross family did not need the money, they followed the other farmers in increasing their production of crops. They just felt that it was the right thing to do to aid the war effort. They offered trees for lumber, cotton for uniforms for the soldiers, and food for the sawmill workers and for those involved in the war effort. They thought that perhaps some of their efforts might help their friends and relatives who were engaged in the conflict.

Will was among the first Americans to land in France after the United States officially entered the war. He was a member of the First Army Division that arrived in France on July 4, 1917. He wrote to his Grandfather regularly, describing their march through Paris and the cheers of the French people. Ben saved all of his letters and shared them with the Rosses. Both families read everything they could find about the war.

Sim could see that all the worry was taking its toll on Ben. Sim was now in his seventies, but even Ben was well along in his sixties. Ben sometimes felt a little guilty about worrying Sim with his troubles so much. Sim, however, assured Ben that he wanted him to share his worries with him and his family. Not too many days passed that these two men did not get together to share their thoughts about what was happening to the American troops in Europe. They both knew of several local young men who were involved in the conflict, but the war to them mainly meant Will and his well-being.

Min was growing older and was not as strong as she used to be, so Queenie began to take over the household chores as well as feeding the stock and the chickens. She did the best she could to keep a garden planted, but her duties were becoming very heavy. Sim was turning more and more of the financial business over to Queenie as well. They made very few trips to Traders Hill because Min could not be left alone, and Queenie would not allow her father to go by himself. So they left the money management up to Henry and his banking assistants, but even Henry had to give up most of his work, due to his own failing health.

Min did not live to see the war's end. As she became weaker, she spent most of her days in bed, and Sim knew that she needed to see a doctor. He finally persuaded her to let him and Queenie take her down to St. George to be examined by a doctor there. The doctor gave her some strong medicine and advised her to get plenty of bed rest. He feared that a stroke was eminent. He told her this fact, and she promised to follow his instructions, but she became worse as each day passed. She died quietly one night in her sleep.

Sim and Queenie sent word to the LaFlours and the Clarks by an early fisherman who happened to be close by, and these friends came immediately. Before they left St. George, they sent word to Mae's family and other friends, as well as to those on the outside. Mae and Mattie took charge of the arrangements because Sim and Queenie were too grieved to make any plans together. Ben and Bo saw to the making of the casket, and they made the grave ready for the funeral.

As was the custom of swamp folk, food was brought in. Mae and Mattie attended to the feeding of all those who were present, while Queenie remained close to her grieving father. Queenie was grieving, too, but she realized how old her father was and how difficult Min's death was for him. He could not stop the tears that streamed from his tired old eyes. Queenie wondered how he could live without his beloved wife. She had been the light of his life, and now that light had been extinguished. Queenie vowed to do the best she could for him, but she knew that life would never again have the same meaning for her beloved Pa.

Min was buried in the little family cemetery with her relatives and many friends standing beside Sim and Queenie. As the mourners gradually left Ross Island, Ben and Mae, as well as Bo and Mattie, insisted on remaining overnight to help clear up the house and do what they could for Sim and Queenie. While these friends attended to these needs, Sim and Queenie returned to the little family cemetery. There they could be alone with Min, Mr. Jim, and Miss Aggie. To them, this was the most sacred spot in the world, the place where the Ross family would all some day rest in peace.

During the days that followed, Ben was a constant visitor. He knew that Sim needed him, but he needed Sim as well. The war in Europe had become worse. The French, British, Belgian, and American troops were fighting hard to stop the Germans, who had advanced within forty miles of Paris. The First Division was among those sent to stop the German drive. Ben had not heard from Will in a long time, but he knew from the newspaper reports that Will's division was fighting the Germans in that massive drive to reach Paris.

Ben went to see Sim hoping for consolation from his good friend. Sim welcomed Ben as he came up the run. He knew that Ben had not heard from Will in a very long time, but he hoped that this visit meant that he had heard from his grandson. Ben handed Sim the latest newspaper. As Sim read, he realized that Will had been in the midst of the very worst fighting. Queenie joined her father in reading the account of the war.

"I'm worryin' myself sick over that boy, Sim. It sounds like pure slaughter over there. I just can't bear to think of Will's being in the midst of all this," said Ben. "If I could just get a letter from him, it would help."

"Will don't have time to write, Ben. He's busy day and night. It's all he can do to keep himself alive," answered Sim. "We'll just have to hope and pray that we'll soon have some good news about that boy."

Sim tried to get Ben's mind off the war by telling him that he and Queenie would soon be going to St. George to order a tombstone for Min's grave. They wanted Ben to help them select the marker. Ben agreed to help, and they set a date for the trip to St. George. Ben insisted that Sim and Queenie stay with him and Mae for a few days. Queenie backed up Ben in this plan, and Sim finally agreed.

The visit seemed to help Sim. Ben and Mae's daughter, Mary, was at home for a visit. She had her two teen-age children with her, a boy and a girl, and they seemed to have a special interest in Queenie. Mary had always had much affection for Queenie, so she was pleased that her children felt the same way.

Mary knew that some day, when Sim passed away, Queenie would be left alone in the swamp. She knew that Ben would never allow Queenie to remain by herself in so isolated an area. Mary loved the town of Folkston, where she and her family now lived. It was growing fast, and she thought that Queenie might like to buy a nice house there one day.

Mary brought the subject up one day when she and Queenie were walking down to a nearby store.

"Queenie," Mary said, "I've been thinkin' about you a lot lately since Miss Min died. In fact, Pa and I have discussed an idea. If your Pa passes away and you are ever left alone down at your place, I hope you will agree to move out of the swamp, hopefully to Folkston. It's a more modern town, and there are some nice houses there. We would be close by to look after you."

"Thank you, Mary," answered Queenie. "I know Pa is gettin' old, but he's right strong. I believe he'll live to be a very old man. I'll be takin' good care of him, and maybe he'll be here a long time. I wouldn't be afraid to stay at our place alone, anyway. We have dogs, and I'm a good shot. In fact, not many folks in the swamp can outshoot me. I do thank you, though, and if the time comes that I'm left alone, I'll think on what you've said."

The subject did not arise again during their visit to the LaFlours, but Mary and Queenie both felt better after their discussion. Queenie could not imagine ever leaving the Ross place. She was not afraid of man or beast. That was her home, and she hoped to live there forever. On the other hand, of course, if she was ever unable to take care of herself, she was glad to know that there was a place where she could go for help. One good thing was that she would never have to worry about money. She knew she would always be able to support herself, so she determined not to worry about the future at that time. Her mission in life, as she could see it, was to take care of her Pa and keep their home going. She knew that Sim would never agree to leave their home. Anyway, she had no desire to leave, either.

When they finally headed back to the swamp, and they were slowly paddling their way up toward their landing, Sim brought up the subject of Queenie's being left alone. Ben had talked to him about the same matter that Mary had discussed with Queenie.

"If you are left alone at our homeplace, Queenie, I want you to leave the swamp. Ben thinks you might move to St. George, but he says that Mary thinks you would be better off at Folkston near her and her family. I think that would be better. She is younger than you are, and Ben and Mae are gettin' old now themselves. I don't ever want to leave our place, but I do not want you down here alone."

"Well, Pa, I don't want you to worry about me, so I'll take your advice. I plan, though, on your being around for a long time. Just keep that in mind, and let's not worry about anything right now, because you know that I'm able to take care of myself," she said.

"Yes, I know. I know, Queenie. And for that I am very grateful," Sim assured her.

They skimmed over the lake in silence and finally pulled out the poles as they reached their run. Out of habit, Sim put his hand up to his mouth to give the holler that they were approaching the house. He suddenly stopped, lowered his hand, and wiped a tear from his eye. There was no need for a holler. There was nobody to hear or answer him. Queenie understood and said nothing.

Chapter Sixteen

☾

The war in Europe ended on November 11, 1918. The entire country rejoiced, but Ben could not bring himself to join in the festivities until he heard from Will.

After several weeks had passed, Sim heard Ben's familiar holler down on the run. He and Queenie rushed out to meet Ben and ask if he had any news of his grandson. A happy Ben reported that he had indeed heard from Will, who was alive and well but would not be home for some time. He would be serving in the Army of Occupation in Germany.

"I don't mind that," said Ben. "Just as long as he is alive and well, I can wait for him to come home. I just hope I live to see him again."

"Oh, you will, Ben. I know you will," answered Sim. "We're so happy about the good news. You'll be hearin' more from him all the time now, I feel sure."

Queenie was so happy that she hugged Ben and cried for joy at the same time.

"I'll tell you one thing, my friends," said Ben. "As soon as I know when he'll be arriving home, I'll catch the next train for Mayday. Mae says she'll be doin' the same. Of course, from his letter it sounds like he may be a long time gettin' back, but I can wait, now that I know he'll be comin' home one of these days. That boy will have lots to tell when he does get home."

"That's right, Ben. We'll all be anxious to see him. I hope he comes down to see all of us when he gets home," added Sim.

"Oh, I know he will," said Ben. "Our children and grandchildren can't wait to see him, either."

Ben soon returned to his home, promising to let them know any further news that he received. Sim and Queenie were so thankful that Will had survived the war. They had grieved to see Ben so anxious for his grandson and were relieved that he could at last settle down and wait for Will to come home, no matter how long it might take.

Queenie was glad to see her Pa take such an interest in Ben's good fortune. Although he had been worried about Will, most of the time he just sat on the front porch and stared into space or walked down to Min's grave. Queenie wished he would not go there so often, but she said nothing. Maybe it helped him to visit Min's grave, but Queenie felt that it only magnified his sorrow. Outside of Ben's anxiety about Will, Sim did not seem interested in much of anything. She had to remind him to eat, and she also told him when he should go to bed and rest. Queenie missed her mother very much, but she worried about her father's detachment from the life around him.

Queenie wondered what she could do to bring him out of his depression. She finally suggested a trip to Traders Hill. Since they still had a key to Henry's house there, they could even stay overnight if Sim felt that the trip was too much for one day. At first, Sim said that he was not up to it. But Queenie reminded him that there had been a long, dry spell, and the horses could get through without any trouble. She insisted that she needed to do some shopping at Traders Hill and told him she would not go alone.

Sim finally agreed to the trip, and they set out early one morning through the eastern edge of the swamp. Queenie had prepared food for the trip and secretly took along their night clothes so that they would not have to hurry back. They had not been to Traders Hill in such a long time, and she was anxious to see how it had changed. She thoughtfully left a note on the front door for Ben, just in case he might come up to see them while they were gone.

When they cleared the boggy area of the swamp and reached the river road, the going was very pleasant. Sim seemed to perk up, and he commented on how beautiful the river was in the early sunlight.

When they were just outside of Traders Hill, Queenie insisted that they go out to Henry's house, rest a while, and have lunch. They found everything there in good order and decided to spend the night. In the meantime, they would go into town and buy some much-needed supplies.

Queenie thought the shopping area seemed a bit run down. Several houses along the way were vacant, evidently because so many people had decided to relocate to Folkston or other nearby towns.

After several hours of shopping and looking around the stores, they returned to the house, ate some of the food that was left from lunch, and succumbed to a good night's rest. The following morning, Sim seemed to feel better than he had in a long time. Queenie prepared him a good breakfast, left a note for Henry saying they had been there, locked up the house, fed and watered the horses, and then they started for home.

Sim was a little tired when they got home, but he insisted that the trip had been good for him. Queenie knew that she had done the right thing by getting him away from home for a day. She realized that the best thing to do was to see that her Pa took short trips on a regular basis to get away from his memories as much as possible.

Besides these short day trips to nearby towns, Queenie insisted that they continue to attend church. They had not attended since Min's illness and death. Queenie felt that seeing his church friends and taking part in the services would help her father. This proved to be true, and Sim was soon almost back to his former self. He could not get around as well as he had once been able to, but he was a tough old swamper who refused to give up or succumb to old age. Sim's determination pleased Queenie, and she did all she could to encourage him to continue with the fishing and hunting that had always been a part of his life.

Even though the war was over, the sawmill business did not slow down. The country was entering a period of general prosperity, and more houses and businesses were being built every day.

Queenie decided to resume her sales to the lumber camps. Vegetables were in demand, as were chickens, eggs, and meat. Sim was gradually becoming more able to help her produce goods for sale, and when he accompanied her to the lumber camps, he took a renewed interest in the news of the day. He visited Ben and his family more often, and Ben was happy to see his friend making a comeback from his sorrow.

As time passed, Ben became impatient with Will's absence. Mae insisted that he try to be more patient, and he did his best, but the waiting was not easy for him. After several months, they finally had a long letter from Will in which he wrote that he hoped to get home early in 1920. That, however, was not all. Apparently he had married a beautiful German girl and would be bringing her home with him. Ben was so excited that he could not wait to give the good news to Sim and Queenie.

When Sim heard Ben's holler, he could tell even before he reached the landing that he had big news, and he and Queenie rejoiced with their friend. Ben would still have a long wait, but this good news made all the waiting worthwhile.

America was experiencing an economic boom by the early 1920s. These years were called the "Golden Twenties." Southeast Georgia was caught up in these good years that followed the close of the war in Europe. Those devastated European countries had to be rebuilt, and the United States profited in this rebuilding. The swampers continued their lives as usual, but people on the outside were spending money as fast as they made it.

In the midst of this boom, Will returned home with his wife, Hulda. As Ben and Mae had planned, they took the first train for Mayday when they knew Will and his wife were coming. Days of happiness and celebration followed. The handsome boy who went away to war was now a handsome man, and his wife, Hulda, was indeed a very beautiful woman.

Hulda was fascinated by everything she saw. She could not speak much English, but Will had taught her enough to carry on a conversation of broken English and German. She charmed the whole family and everyone she met on the farm.

Will told his grandfather that he had saved most of the money he had earned while he was stationed in Germany, and he hoped to take Hulda and his Aunt Sari on a train trip out west before they settled down to farming. He and Hulda had taken a trip from Germany over to Switzerland for their honeymoon, and he now wanted to show Hulda some of her new country and take his aunt on a trip out west he promised her long ago.

Before the trip, however, he planned to take Hulda to St. George to meet the rest of Ben's family and friends. He was especially looking forward to showing Hulda the famous Okefenokee Swamp and introducing her to his friends, Sim and Queenie Ross.

Will followed through on his plans, and after their trip out West, he and Hulda settled down to a life of farming. Eventually he developed a very prosperous tobacco farm, and the LaFlour farm once again became a profitable enterprise.

Before too long, Will bought one of the new automobiles that had recently come on the market. Hulda could not believe all of the luxury she had found as Will's wife. She loved everything about the farm, she loved Will's family, especially his Aunt Sari, and she loved America.

While all the changes and excitement were taking place in the LaFlour family, Sim and Queenie continued their life as usual. Sim was doing quite well in spite of his age, and Queenie took good care of her Pa and tried to keep him healthy. During the good times of the 1920s, Sim was advancing toward his eighties, but—tough old man that he was—he showed very little change in his health. By that time, Queenie was well into her fifties, but her age did not bother her. She was able to attend to her duties and take care of her Pa's needs. They fished, hunted, grew vegetables, sold produce to the sawmillers, and attended church and local sings together. Her days were filled, and she asked for nothing more.

Henry and Harry Cooper were both gone by then, but Sim and Queenie did not worry about their money at St. Marys. Ben, however, did worry some about the country's economic situation. He and his son, Jed, had checked on the bank at St. Marys when Henry died, but they had found nothing to be concerned about. However, because Ben was a good business man, he realized that people were spending too much money and taking too many chances in the stock market and in the business world.

Ben approached Sim and Queenie with these worries, and he told them that he was concerned about the solvency of the banks. He said that he and Jed had decided to invest most of their money in wooded land and farm land outside the swamp. There was more land to be had in southeast Georgia and north Florida, and Ben suggested that Sim put much of his money in the purchase of some of this land. If the banks should fail, at least they would not lose what they had.

Sim and Queenie listened to Ben's advice and made plans to follow it. Ben agreed to take them to St. Marys and consult the bankers there about this matter. Ben knew that much of the Rosses' wealth was tied up in swamp land, which was a good investment because timber was always in demand. But when Sim told Ben how much money he had in the bank at St. Marys, Ben was more convinced than ever that Sim should move at least some of it elsewhere.

Mary's husband, David McClure, was prospering in the turpentine business and had begun investing in real estate in and around Folkston. Ben suggested that Sim might like to do the same and perhaps move some of his money up to the Folkston bank. David was buying up property for Ben and Jed and agreed to do the same for Sim and Queenie.

They made the trip to St. Marys, and both Ben and Jed accompanied their friends and helped them to make wise decisions about their finances. It turned out to be not only a business trip, but an exciting pleasure trip for Queenie and Sim as well. They spent several days at St. Marys and had an enjoyable visit. They returned by way of Folkston and spent the night there with Mary and her family.

When Sim and Queenie finally returned home, they found settling down difficult after the excitement of their trip. But the quiet Ross land was home, and that was where they belonged.

Before too long, Sim and Queenie were to be more grateful than ever for the help their friends had given them. In 1927, a devastating hurricane hit Miami. Hundreds and hundreds of people were killed, and the storm caused millions of dollars in property damage. Before the area could recover from this disaster, a terrible economic depression hit the entire country. In 1929, the stock market crashed, and the business world was thrown into chaos. Banks failed all over the United States, and people who had been wealthy were broke overnight. The banks at St. Marys and Folkston held, but that was not true of those in most of the country.

Chapter Seventeen

☾

As the Great Depression of the 1930s spread over the entire country, southeast Georgia was not spared. Even though the Ross and LaFlour families did not lose the money they still had in the banks, the timber was no longer selling very well because most people did not have money for building. The two families remained in constant dread that the banks would eventually close and they would lose their money. They held on to their land and believed that the wealth they had in trees and land would not be lost.

The logging business did not die completely because railroads still had to buy cypress logs for crossties. This income supported Sim's and Ben's families, so they did not worry too much about the hard times. They did worry, however, about the poverty that they saw all around them, and they helped those in need whenever they could do so.

For Sim and Queenie, a new problem began to worry them. Back in 1919, the Georgia General Assembly passed a bill asking the federal government to make the Okefenokee Swamp a national park. This bill was never acted upon, but now, in the 1930s, there was a new rumor that the federal government in Washington might actually take over the swamp and declare it a National Wildlife Refuge. Many people on the outside urged the federal government to take over the area and preserve the plants and wildlife found there.

Sim and Ben discussed this rumor, but Sim felt that there was no need to worry. Back in the early part of the century, a large lumber company had settled in the north swamp and cut valuable timber, and after eighteen years, this company had finally closed and moved out. Since then, other people had made several unsuccessful attempts to drain the swamp and build canals, but each time, these plans had failed. Sim felt that this new idea of the government taking over the Okefenokee was simply a foolish rumor and would be as unsuccessful as all of the other attempts to take over the swamp.

"I hope you are right, Sim," said Ben. "There are many families who have reared several generations in this swamp, just as you and your family have. I can't see how the government can come in and push all of them, including you, out of their homes."

Sim agreed with him, but Queenie was not so sure. She kept quiet on the matter, however, because she did not want to worry her Pa.

These rumors quieted down somewhat, and life in the swamp continued as usual until one of the worst fires in the history of the area engulfed a large area of the swamp in 1932. They had gone almost completely without rain for a long time. The grass, the peat moss, and even the trees and bushes were dried out beyond safety. Many people believed that the fire had been set accidentally by someone being careless with a lighted match. Others believed that lightning had set off the blaze. Whatever the cause, the fire burned and smoldered until the entire swamp was affected. Where there was no actual flame, the smoke engulfed everything until life in the area was almost unbearable.

The blaze did not reach the Ross place, but heavy smoke could be seen not too far in the distance. Sim and Queenie watched the advance of the flaming inferno and kept their boats ready to leave for the outside at a moment's notice, if necessary.

Sim and Queenie knew that much of their timber would be ruined. Sim assured his daughter that the timber would soon be replenished. "I have seen Okefenokee fires from time to time during my whole life, Queenie," he said, "and the rich land we're on will soon bring it all back."

"But, Pa," said Queenie, "I believe this is the worst fire to ever hit the swamp."

"It is bad," admitted Sim, "but everything will come right back. The smoke is bad, but I just hope it don't get to our house. Let's just don't worry. As soon as the rain comes, we'll be safe."

The rain did come, torrents of it. The fires ceased, and Sim and Queenie settled back down to their regular routine. They went out to inspect the devastation and found that it was worse than they had originally thought. Much of the land was completely barren—the pitcher plants, the beautiful water lilies, the hooray plants, and thousands of pine and cypress trees were all blackened. Queenie felt like crying when she saw the destruction. Sim, however, did not seem too worried. He emphasized that this was nature's way of refreshing and replenishing the swamp. "Don't worry about it, Queenie," Sim said soothingly. "It will all come back in time."

"But, Pa, think of all the timber we've lost!"

"Well, Queenie, just think of it this way: the timber is not in much demand now, and burning out the underbrush will help the trees that come along later."

"I'm glad, Pa, that you can take this with such good spirits."

"There's another thing to remember. We didn't lose our house, the horses, chickens, pigs, or our barn or outhouse."

"I know, Pa. You're such a good man to accept things as they are. I wish I was more like you."

Sure enough, as the 1930s moved along, the swamp became green again. The trees and the vegetation that were charred came alive again with greenery, and many of the swamp plants came back. Most of the animals had somehow managed to survive, and the swamp was once again a place of beauty. Even the swaying Spanish moss resumed its place on the trees and swayed in the gentle breezes. The world seemed right once more, even though the rest of the country continued to suffer the Great Depression.

When Franklin D. Roosevelt became President of the United States, some people from the North once again became interested in the swamp. They placed much value on the plants and animals that were found there, and they appealed to President Roosevelt to declare the Okefenokee swamp a wildlife refuge so that these gifts of nature could be protected. The animals, in particular, were being depleted at an alarming rate. The bears and alligators had been destroyed in great numbers, in part for the pleasure of hunters who were coming into the swamp from the outside. The swampers themselves killed these animals for food and to supplement their livelihood. Bears were some of the worst predators, because they killed hogs and chickens in great numbers. Many swampers hunted them regularly and hung their skulls on their fences. To them, the killing of bears was simply a way of protecting their food supply and livestock. Swampers hunted alligators and sold the hides to augment their family's income. This was the swamper's home, and he supported his family in the same manner that his forefathers had supported their families. The outsiders who came in and exploited the animals without discrimination were another problem, but the swampers felt that there was little they could do about the situation.

In 1937, President Roosevelt listened to his friends and, by executive order, created the Okefenokee Wildlife Refuge from parts of Ware, Charlton, and Clinch counties. When the swamp became federal property, many of the families began to move out. Some of them moved to the small towns surrounding the swamp, but many moved as far away as Atlanta, Savannah, Macon, Brunswick, Waycross, and Valdosta. Most of the swampers had never thought that this day would come, and when it finally did, most of them found the adjustment difficult.

As soon as Ben heard this news, he went immediately to see Sim and Queenie. Sim seemed unconcerned, but Queenie was especially worried about how this would affect her Pa. He had not been feeling very well in the past few months. He slept a great deal and was growing more confused in his thinking. He was, after all, in his nineties now. Queenie knew that his mind was more alert than that of most people at his age, but she still avoided worrying him as much as she could.

Ben did tell Sim about the plans for the government takeover, but he made it sound as though there was nothing about which to worry. To Queenie, however, he explained the full impact of the situation. He did not know how it would affect the Rosses, but he assured her that he felt they would be fully compensated for any land that the government took. He also felt that there would be no rush for them to move out and advised her to carry on life as usual there on the Ross island. He told her that he and Jed planned to go to Folkston within a few days and confer with his son-in-law, David, and perhaps a good lawyer concerning the full impact of this decision by the government. Ben himself owned quite a bit of timberland in the swamp, so the government plans would affect him as well as Sim and Queenie, although not to as great an extent.

Queenie decided not to worry about the situation. Anyone would have a hard time trying to make her leave her home until she was good and ready. Most importantly, she had to keep her Pa from worrying. She decided the federal government could do what they wanted, but they'd just better leave her and her Pa alone.

Ben went up to see Sim and Queenie the day after he returned from Folkston. "There's something you have to get accustomed to, Queenie. You can't shoot any of the animals on government land. They haven't got the whole refuge straightened out yet, but they're workin' on it. That means you can't go huntin' or shootin' the animals."

"Oh, that won't be possible, Ben," said Queenie adamantly. "They'd kill all our chickens and every last hog we have. Them hogs ain't no match for them long bear claws."

"I know, Queenie, and that's worryin' me, too. We can't shoot the alligators or anything else on government land. We can live with that, I guess, but I don't see how swampers can exist if they can't protect their food supply. They'll be federal people patrolling all up and down these lakes and runs to check on poachers," Ben added.

While Ben and Queenie were talking on the front porch, they suddenly heard a peculiar sound coming from Sim's room. They immediately went to the bed where he was resting. He was awake but confused in his speech. After they talked with him for a while, he finally grew clearer in his thinking. Ben talked to him while Queenie carried him a glass of fresh milk.

Ben decided that he had better go home and bring help for Queenie. He was not satisfied with Sim's condition, so he decided to bring Mae and maybe Mattie as well. Ben knew that Sim may have had a slight stroke, and he also knew that he could have another, stronger stroke at any time. Queenie agreed to Ben's plan, and Ben left for St. George.

Queenie did not sleep that night but instead kept a close vigil over her beloved Pa. He was breathing very easily, and she began to think that perhaps he was getting over the upset of the previous afternoon. Around dawn, she went into the kitchen to make him a good breakfast. He was able to eat some of the food but soon fell asleep again. Queenie was not hungry. She just sat by his bed and drank coffee.

"Lord," she prayed, "please help our friends to come soon. I don't think I can face Pa's leaving here all by myself."

About that time, she heard Ben, Mae, and Mattie on the front porch. They had not given the swamp holler this time. They knew they were expected, and they didn't want to disturb Sim if he happened to be awake. They felt relieved when Queenie walked up the hall and told them that her Pa was resting comfortably. Mae and Mattie had packed their small bags, so Queenie knew that they planned to stay as long as they were needed.

Sim died quietly in the middle of the morning. Queenie and her three friends were sitting by his bed, watching his breathing become more and more labored. Without any warning, he opened his eyes, and in a clear voice said, "Min, is that you, Honey? Wait for me, Min!" Then he closed his eyes and simply stopped breathing. Queenie and her friends stood by his bedside and saw his wrinkles seem to fade away. He looked young again. Somehow they knew he was with his beloved Min once again.

Ben checked him to be sure there was no heartbeat. Queenie leaned over and kissed her Pa, and Mae and Mattie did the same. All three women placed their arms around each other and wept. Ben stood for a very long time, just looking down at his old friend. "Goodbye, Sim," he said. "Goodbye, my good friend, until we meet again. I'll miss you for as long as I live."

Mae and Mattie told Ben to take Queenie from the room so that they could attend to the body. Queenie told them, however, that there was something she must get for them. She went to the storage room and brought out a box.

"This here is Pa's Confederate uniform," she said. "Grandma, Ma, and I have kept it in good condition all these years. Please put it on him. I promised Ma I would see that this is done. The Confederate flag is in the box, too. We'll put that on his coffin."

Queenie then walked out with Ben. He told Mae that he would go home and tell their relatives and friends the news about Sim. He would also secure for them a ready-made casket. He left quietly, promising to return as soon as possible. While Mae and Mattie were busy in Sim's room, Queenie sat quietly on the front porch and talked to her Pa.

"Well, Pa," she said, "I know it was time for you to go be with Ma, Grandma, and Grandpa. You were such a good man that I know God will see that you are happy forever. I don't know what I'll do, but I'll manage, Pa. I know I will. We here in the swamp are tough folks, so don't you worry about me none. Just be happy there in Heaven, Pa. Just be happy, 'cause you deserve to be happy forever."

People came from all parts of the swamp, as well as from the outside, to pay tribute to this renowned old swamper. Here was a man who had not harmed his neighbors, who had lived life to the fullest, and had loved and taken care of his family. As those who were present gazed upon the old swamper in his ancient Confederate uniform, many shed tears for the lost cause of the Confederacy, as well as for the loss of their friend.

The flag-draped coffin was carried down to the Ross family cemetery by Ben, Bo, and several other friends. Mae and Mattie walked beside Queenie, and they were followed by at least a hundred friends. Everyone paid their respects to one of the last real old-time swampers. Even though times were changing, this man had not changed. He stood resolutely for the love and freedom of the people who knew what freedom was all about.

After the Confederate flag was folded and handed to Queenie, she held it close to her heart. She silently vowed that this flag would never leave her possession as long as she lived.

One by one, their friends slowly left, but the LaFlours and the Clarks remained with Queenie. They would not leave her alone until they knew for certain that she was ready to face the change that must now come into her life.

Chapter Eighteen

☾

After Sim's funeral, the LaFlours and the Clarks remained with Queenie overnight. Mae was not feeling very well, so the following morning, Ben asked that she go on home and rest. Mattie, however, insisted on staying until Bo could find some girl to come and stay with Queenie temporarily, until she got her affairs in order. Queenie tried to assure them that she could remain in her home alone until she could attend to her personal business, but Ben would not hear of it. Ben and Jed promised her that they would accompany her to Folkston to confer with the Department of the Interior about the transfer of her land to the federal reservation and also assist her in purchasing a nice marker for Sim's grave. She planned as well to hire someone to place a strong chain-link fence around the Ross family cemetery. One thing that the federal people must assure her was that the graves of her parents and grandparents would never be disturbed.

Queenie discussed all of these plans with Ben before he left. She had to decide what to do with the horses, chickens, cows, and pigs. She could not simply go off and leave them unattended. She knew that the house, barn, and outhouse would have to be left to the elements, but there were a few pieces of furniture that she would never give up, particularly the beautiful pieces made by Harry Cooper. There was so much to think about. She felt bad that Mattie would be away from her own home for a number of days, but deep down she was grateful for her presence. Mattie had so much common sense, and her advice would be a great help.

Mattie had told Bo of a young black girl she knew who would likely be happy to accept a job helping Queenie full time. This girl was an orphan who lived with relatives who were not very kind to her. They forced her to work very hard without any compensation, except an inadequate place to live and poor food.

Mattie told Queenie about the girl and insisted that Queenie hire either her or some other person to help her. Mainly, Mattie thought that Queenie just needed someone else in the house. At first, Queenie politely refused, but Mattie's insistence made her realize that perhaps this was a good idea.

"Miss Queenie, you know that you'll have to be goin' to the outside before too long. I believe this girl would be willin' to move with you to Folkston or wherever you go. She got nothin' or nobody, and I believe she's honest. So if Bo's able to talk this girl—her name's Genie Hall—into workin' for you, I believe she'd be a good person for you to hire."

"I know you're tryin' to help, Mattie, but I don't see why I can't just stay here by myself."

"Because this swamp ain't the same no more, Miss Queenie. There's all kinds of dangerous folks around now. If they see you here by yourself, there's no tellin' what they'll do. If they see somebody else here, I know it'll sure make a difference. They won't know just how many folks is exactly here."

"Well, Mattie, you do make sense," admitted Queenie, "but there's no use for her to come down here yet. I've got to go down to St. George before long and get Ben to take me to Folkston to get a tombstone for Pa's grave. I've got to see them government people, too, about paying me for my land. That's valuable timbered land, and they ain't goin' to get it for nothin'."

"You're right to do that first. Bo will be back in a day or so, and we'll have to talk to him about comin' up here and minding your house and your animals while you're away."

"I've been thinkin' about that, Mattie. If you and Bo can use the livestock, I want to give 'em to you. I'll keep the chickens for a while, but I have plenty of cured meat to last me as long as I stay here. I could offer some of my things to the LaFlours, but they wouldn't want any of it. They have everything they need."

"Oh, we couldn't ever repay you for all of that, Miss Queenie!" Mattie protested. "You'll have to sell them animals and make some money to help buy you a house when you leave out of here."

"That won't be necessary, Mattie. I'll manage just fine, 'cause the government will have to give me some money for my land they're takin'. All I ask is that Bo put up a heavy chain fence around our family's cemetery. I'll get the chain shipped over to St. George, and Bo can bring it up here. Do you think he'll agree to that?"

"Oh, Miss Queenie, you know he wouldn't take anythin' to attend to it, and when you do move out, me and Bo will gladly come up here from time to time and check on everythin' on your island for you."

"I'll be thankin' you for that, Mattie. And there's one other thing," added Queenie. "There's a few pieces of furniture that I have to keep, but I want you and Bo to take what's left when I do go to the outside. I know that these people who are comin' down here to check around on the swamp will likely take what's left in the house. If you can't use all of the furniture that's left, just give it to any of your friends who can use it."

"We'll forever be grateful to you, Miss Queenie," said Mattie. "Maybe they'll be some way we can repay you some day."

"No need for that, Mattie. Now, let's just walk down to the buryin' ground and see that everything is all right."

After the two women had freshened up the flowers on Sim's grave, they walked slowly up to the house and sat quietly on the front porch for a long time. There was no need to go out to the kitchen and build a fire in the cookstove to prepare supper. The friends who had brought food when they came to Sim's funeral had brought enough to last for many days. So the women just sat quietly rocking and listening to the noises of the swamp. When the darkness set in and the buzzing of the mosquitoes became unbearable, they entered the ghostly, quiet dwelling to put supper on the table at last.

"I'll tell you, Mattie, you'll never know how much I appreciate your staying with me right now. I don't know how I could have made it if you hadn't been here."

"Thank you, Miss Queenie. I thought you'd need somebody with you. A house is mighty quiet after somebody goes away. I hope I've been of some help to you."

Before Bo came down to check on the ladies at the Ross place, Mattie had almost decided that Queenie really did not need any help in order to remain on her place. She came to this conclusion when the two women were busy in the back part of the house one afternoon, and they heard a boat coming up the run. Queenie immediately picked up her shotgun and went to the front porch. Mattie followed closely and cautiously behind her.

"Stop where you are, Mister!" Queenie commanded. "I don't know who you are, but folks don't come up my run without givin' a clear holler to let me know they're comin'."

"We're government men, Ma'am. We see that there are some bear skulls up on your fence. Don't you know that nobody is allowed to shoot bears in this government reserve now? You're going to land yourself in jail if you keep shootin' these animals down here," warned one of the men.

"Them skulls have been on that fence for years. Besides, this ain't government land just yet. I'll shoot whatever I choose to protect my chickens and pigs. Now, get off my property before I shoot you, too," Queenie ordered defiantly.

The men made no move to turn back. Mattie moved up and stood close beside Queenie, who now raised her gun, cocked it, and pointed it at the occupants of the boat. "I ain't so sure you're government men, anyway," Queenie drawled. "So I'll give you two seconds to get off my property. If you're not gone in that time, I'll blow a hole clean through both of you, and I'll feed what's left to the alligators!"

The men thought she was bluffing, so they made no move to leave the run. At that moment, Queenie shouted, "Duck! There's a chicken hawk right over your head, and I have to get it!"

She shot a resounding blast just above their heads. Both men jumped to duck the shot, and they overturned the boat and landed in the water. As they struggled to set the boat right, Queenie shouted, "There comes another one," and she shot another blast just above their heads again.

The men knew there was no hawk and told her so. But when she raised her shotgun again, they gave her another warning and turned back as fast as possible.

Once they had cleared the run, Queenie lowered her gun. Only then did Mattie relax, and she went into peals of laughter. Queenie joined her and felt that her Pa would be proud of her for letting the strangers know who was in charge of the Ross place.

"I'll tell you, Mattie," laughed Queenie, "I'm not really sure that they *were* federal people. Whoever they are, though, they'd better give us fair warning before they enter the Ross run again."

"I don't want you to stay here by yourself, Miss Queenie, but I do believe that if you did, you could take care of yourself," Mattie replied, admiring her friend.

"Yes, I could, Mattie, but Pa made me promise not to stay out here by myself. But I do believe I really would be happier to go on livin' here."

"You might be, but you know that sooner or later, those government men will stop you from shootin' these animals. I honestly don't see how you could take care of your cow, pigs, and chickens if you can't shoot them bears. For another thing, Miss Queenie, you would be so lonesome out here with all your folks gone. Even if we get Genie to stay with you, it just wouldn't be the same."

Bo came up the following day, and Queenie talked to him about her livestock and offered it to him. He was indeed grateful. "I know the LaFlours don't need anything I have here, so I do hope you can use the stock and the furniture that I don't take with me," offered Queenie.

"Oh, Miss Queenie, I could never repay you for all of this," answered Bo. "But I do know that you just can't move off and leave your stock here with nobody to take care of it."

"I've talked to Mattie about this, Bo, and I told her that what you could do to repay me would be to put up a heavy chain fence around our family graveyard. I'll get' the chain for the fence myself when I go to Folkston."

"I'll be glad to do that for you, Miss Queenie, and anything else I can do. If you really want us to have your stock, I'll bring somebody up with me to ride out the horses through the east swamp. That way, we can lead out the cow at the same time. The pigs and anything else can be hauled down to St. George by boat." He paused, then said, "Oh, Miss Queenie, I did get little Genie to say she would work for you. She's afraid of the swamp, but I told her that you'd be moving out before long."

At that, Mattie began to giggle. "I'm glad she's movin' out, Bo, but don't ever think she can't look after herself." She told Bo about the two men in the boat, and Bo, laughing with her, agreed that Queenie could indeed take care of herself. He said, however, that Mr. Ben was anxious for her to move to the outside as soon as possible. Besides, he knew that she had promised her Pa that she would move and not stay in the swamp alone.

He told her that Mr. Ben had instructed him to bring the two women back with him to St. George. Ben knew that Mattie needed to get back home, and he felt that Queenie needed to get on over to Folkston and attend to her personal business. Ben had made arrangements with Mary and David for himself, Mae, Jed, and Queenie to stay with them while Queenie bought the tombstone for Sim's grave and attended to her settlement with the government agents. Ben had also asked Mary to look around for a house that would be suitable for Queenie. Ben hoped that there would be a place close to Mary, since he felt that Queenie might have a difficult time adjusting to her strange new surroundings.

Queenie, Bo, and Mattie left plenty of food for the horses and the cow, fed the chickens and pigs, and locked up the house as best they could. They chained the Ross boats to a tree, locked them in place, and left for St. George. Bo made plans to return to the Ross place the following day to see about the livestock.

When Queenie arrived in St. George, she learned something that was a little frightening to her. Jed had bought an automobile. There were quite a few of these vehicles in Folkston, and Queenie had seen them before, but she had never actually ridden in one. Jed planned to take Queenie, Ben, and Mae to Folkston in his new car. Queenie could not bring herself to tell Ben and Mae that she was afraid to ride in an automobile. She soon learned, however, that Mae had the same fear, a fact which was some comfort to Queenie.

As tactfully as she could, Mae suggested that they take a day to go shopping before their trip. Queenie had brought some clothes along with her, but the old straw hat she wore and most of her dresses would not be suitable attire for attending to business. Mae suggested that they both go to the little general store at St. George to buy a new dress, maybe two if they had good luck.

Mattie brought Genie over to meet Queenie. She was a very shy young girl, but Queenie was pleased with her and made plans to get to know her better after her trip to Folkston.

When they left for Folkston, Queenie and Mae wore their new dresses and hats, and they looked like real cityfolk. Jed and Ben sat on the front seat of the automobile, and Queenie and Mae occupied the rear seat. As they started down the bumpy road, the two women clutched each other's hands and actually turned quite pale for the first few miles. They both feared that they would have a serious wreck at any minute. But after they covered some distance without any mishap, they decided that perhaps they would not be killed on this ride after all.

Jed and Ben were having a good time. To them, the car was like a shiny new toy. "You know, Jed," said Ben, "I just might buy me one of these contraptions. I think I could handle it all right."

"Well, Pa, I'd rather you didn't, at your age," replied Jed, smiling at his father. "I'll take you anywhere you want to go, but I'm afraid your eyesight is not quite good enough to drive."

When the group reached Folkston, they learned that David had bought himself a car, too, and the biggest surprise of all was that Mary had learned to drive. Upon discovering this news, Queenie and Mae decided that they had just as well accept that in this new, modern world, these automobiles were here to stay.

Chapter Nineteen

☾

Queenie's time at Folkston proved to be very busy. She was able to take care of some of her business there, but Jed advised her to hire a lawyer to settle with the government. The lawyer could go to Waycross, over to Kingsland, or any other town to settle any pending business. Ben and Jed were not satisfied with Queenie's final settlement, but they realized that she would be wise to go ahead and take the offer anyway. Ben met with the same disappointment with the settlement for his own land in the swamp. He knew that he and Queenie had not received enough money for their land, but the government insisted on offering Depression prices. Ben and Jed both felt that they had just as well settle with the government and get this unpleasant business behind them.

They conferred with several of their friends who were moving out of the north swamp, and these people were meeting with the same disappointment. The difference, however, was that Queenie and Ben were well-off financially. They could get along fine with what they had in the banks already. Also, they both owned quite a bit of land outside the swamp, which would not be touched unless they decided to sell some of it themselves.

Queenie had always thought that she knew something about the business world, but she soon learned that her knowledge was very limited. She was so thankful that Ben and Jed were there to advise her. The lawyer that she hired, James Cook, was a young man who proved to be very reliable. Queenie decided that if she moved to Folkston, this young man would likely be a big help in handling her affairs. Swamp people had always attended to their own business, but this new life she was entering was very different from anything she had known before. She wished that she had been better educated, but there had never been an opportunity to learn more than what her parents had taught her. She knew she would just have to trust James Cook. But he was a friend of David, and Queenie believed that any friend of David would certainly be trustworthy.

Queenie's next decision concerned where she should settle. She talked at length with Mae and Mary about this, and both of them felt that Folkston was a better choice than St. George. "I would like for you to live near us at St. George," began Mae, "but the truth is that me and Ben are gettin' on in years. So I'd like to see you settle near Mary and David. Folkston is growing fast, and it's on one of the tourist routes for people goin' to Florida from up north. When you see all these cars goin' through, that's who these folks are."

"I think Mama is right, Queenie," agreed Mary. "If you can make up your mind about where to live, we can be lookin' for a house for you while you're here. There's a good house for sale right down the street from us. Mama says you're likely to hire Genie Hall to help you, and there's a nice little house in the back yard of that place where Genie could live. She'd be there to help you and still have her own privacy, too. If you're interested, we can go down there and look at the place."

Queenie agreed to go look, but when she saw what a nice place it was, she insisted that it was too fine for her. She thought about her home in the swamp and believed that she would never be able to adjust to such luxury.

Mary, however, refused to give up. "Other swampers are making the same adjustments, Queenie. Maybe they're not moving into places as luxurious as this, but they are changing their ways to live on the outside. The difference is that you don't have to worry about money, and most of them are poor. You're lucky because your Pa and Grandpa were smart enough to think ahead and buy up rich timberland. You can depend on me to help you get settled, Queenie. We could have a good time together. I've been missing my children, since they've married and moved to Florida. If you'd come here and let me help you, that would give me something to do. You'll be surprised how many swampers have settled in this area. Lots of them even go to my church."

Queenie looked around her and sighed. "I know this is the place where I should settle, Mary, but I don't think I could ever get accustomed to all these cars and all these Yankees comin' through all the time. You're right about my having money, but I can't imagine paying ten thousand dollars for a house!"

"David and I looked at this house last week, and he thought the price was reasonable. He's anxious for you to settle near us, too. He can be of great help to you in handling your business affairs."

"Well, I'll think about it, Mary. I know I'd get to see you and Mae and Ben from time to time, and Jed and his wife, Sallie, when they come up to visit you and David."

"To tell you the truth, Queenie," said Mae, "I believe that sooner or later, Jed and Sallie will move to Folkston themselves. This town is up and comin', but St. George is off the beaten path. In fact, I doubt if it will ever grow much larger. Of course, we'll always live there, 'cause we have our nice house there, but so many of the younger generation have already moved out. I doubt if me and Ben could ever adjust to any other place. In your case, though, you don't really have a choice. You have to go some place."

Queenie knew they were right, but she just didn't know what to do. She decided to talk to Ben. He was the closest person to her Pa that she knew. She had always depended on Pa's advice, and now she must turn to Ben. He would know what she should do.

Queenie did talk to Ben, and he went with her to see the house in question. He liked it and pointed out the fact that the church she would likely attend was only two blocks away, and the town's shopping area was within walking distance, as well.

"But, Ben," Queenie protested, "I can't imagine paying ten thousand dollars for a house! What do you think Pa would say about spending that much just for a place to live?"

"Well, Queenie," answered Ben, "to tell you the truth, I think he'd tell you to go ahead and settle down in that house. I wish we'd insisted that you and your father move over here while he was still here to advise you."

"That would have been a good thing, I think, but you know there was no way we could've talked Pa into moving out of the swamp. To be honest," Queenie laughed, "I think all of this noise, and smelling the paint on the houses, and having to wear shoes all the time would have worried him to death. It's gonna be hard enough for me to adjust, but after he got so old, I just don't think there was any way he could've been satisfied on the outside."

"I know exactly what you mean. I've been talkin' to some of the old swampers from the north swamp who've moved here. They tell me that they've been havin' a hard time settlin' down. The young folks don't seem to worry too much about coming to the outside. It's just the old folks who aren't too happy here."

"Well, if you think this house is the best place for me, I'll take your advice. I do like the fact that Genie can have her own house in the back yard. I can do my own housework right now, but as I get older, I may need somebody to help me. I guess it would be a good thing for me to train her to cook and keep house while I'm still able to show her what to do. For another thing, I do feel sorry for her. She's a pitiful little thing, and Mattie tells me that she's had a hard time where she's been livin'. I guess the Christian thing to do is take her in and help her as much as I can."

"You know, Queenie, Mary's cook, Matilda, will gladly take her to the black folk's church, and to functions in the black community."

"And if there's a school here for black children," added Queenie, "I'd want her to go to school, too. But I guess I'll worry about that later."

When Queenie and Ben returned to Mary's home, Queenie told everyone that she had decided to buy the house, on the condition that Mary and David help her decide what furniture she needed and show her where to buy it. Of course, Mary and David happily assured her that they would help her in any way they could, and Queenie told Mary that she would need her help to buy some new clothes, as well. "Except for the dresses and the new hat that Mae helped me pick out at St. George, my clothes just don't look fittin' for the city. The folks I see on the streets here wear a different kind of clothes. I don't want folks pointin' me out as some old swamp woman when I walk down the street."

"Don't you worry about that, Queenie," laughed Mary. "There are too many swamp people movin' here now. But I'll certainly be glad to help you buy some new clothes. We might even go up to Waycross or over to Kingsland and do some shopping there. We can have a good time doing that and buying furniture for your house."

The following day, with the help of David and James Cook, Queenie bought the house. With their business in order and the visit with Mary and David completed, Ben, Jed, Mae, and Queenie returned to St. George. Queenie admitted to Mae and Ben that while she was thankful that she'd settled her business and bought the house, she was afraid to live on the outside. She didn't know if she'd ever adjust, or if she'd get along well with the people and become a part of the community. It was all so strange and new to her. Mae and Ben assured her that Mary and David would see that all went well for her.

Ben took Queenie up to her home in the swamp, and little Genie Hall accompanied them. They could all tell that Genie was afraid. When she saw a snake near the boat as they poled their way up the run, she let out a blood-curdling scream. Ben grabbed a paddle and swiftly demolished the reptile.

"Don't be afraid, Genie," said Queenie. "We're not gonna let you get hurt."

"Oh, Miss Queenie!" cried Genie. "I'm afraid of this swamp! I done heard too many stories about how folks gets killed by snakes and alligators out here!"

"Well, just try not to worry, 'cause we'll be movin' over to Folkston before you know it."

"I don't know where that is, but I'll be glad to go there if it ain't in the swamp," said Genie.

Ben laughed. "Oh, you'll like that town, Genie. You and Miss Queenie are goin' to have a real pretty place to live in. Now, try not to worry Miss Queenie by screaming every time you see a bug or an animal. They won't hurt you, and the more you help Miss Queenie pack up her belongings, the sooner you'll be leavin' the swamp."

"I can pack, Mr. Ben," Genie assured him. "I can pack real fast."

When Ben was preparing to leave, Queenie asked him to wait one week before returning for her and Genie. She wanted to take her time in deciding what she would take with her and what she would leave for Mattie and Bo. She also suggested that he ask Mattie and Bo to come up with him when he returned to take her and Genie back to St. George. Queenie wanted to be sure that they got the chickens and the furniture she did not take with her. Ben agreed and assured her that they would all help her and Genie move to their new home in Folkston.

As planned, Mattie and Bo brought their large boat to the Ross place on the appointed day, and Ben followed them in his own boat. Bo planned to load his large boat with the heavy furniture, and Ben would use his boat for any smaller household items. He and Queenie both thought that they should leave as little as possible for the pillagers who were sure to follow them.

Queenie and Genie had things in such good order that the loading did not take long. Genie was moving with extra speed. She knew the faster she worked, the sooner she would be out of the swamp. Queenie could not help being amused at her new friend.

Queenie, on the other hand, was not moving very fast at all. She knew she was leaving behind a whole lifetime of memories and dreams. She was leaving the people she loved most in the world. She was glad they were at rest, but she knew now that she would never rest beside them. She had no idea how much longer she would live or how well she would adjust to her new life on the outside.

When it was almost time to leave, Queenie walked alone down to the family cemetery. She was glad to see that the four graves looked very secure with the heavy chain fence around them. Bo had built a gate for easy entrance to the little cemetery, and this gate was secured by a heavy lock. Queenie was very pleased with the good job he'd done. She took out the only key, slowly unlocked the gate, and stepped inside the sacred place.

"Well, Pa, Ma, Grandma, and Grandpa, I'll be goin' now. It seems the only thing I can do. The government people promised me that your graves would always be protected, and I'll come back from time to time to check on you. I think everything will be all right, and I'll do the best I can to make a good life for myself on the outside. I wish I could stay here on our homeplace, but I know that can't be. Now, you remember that I love you all, and I'll miss you as long as I live."

She kissed each stone marker, locked the gate, and walked slowly up to the house. The boats were loaded and sitting in the run, and Queenie's friends waited respectfully while she took one last look inside the house. It was vacant now, and without the furniture, it no longer looked the same. She walked down to the run with tears on her cheeks, climbed into the boat, and took her place beside Genie. She picked up her poles, cleared her throat, and said, "All right. I'm ready now."

Genie reached over and patted Queenie's hand. The little black girl said nothing, but she knew that in this old woman beside her, she had found love and consideration that she had never known before.

Chapter Twenty

☾

The move to Folkston proved to be much smoother than Queenie had dared to hope, in part because she had a great deal of help. Ben borrowed one of the lumber company wagons to haul her scant furniture and personal belongings to her new home, and Mae even rode along with him back to Folkston to help. Jed, Sallie, Ben, Mae, and Queenie went in Jed's automobile. Genie, however, insisted on riding with Bo, who was driving the wagon. She wanted no part of that dangerous automobile.

After the wagon was unloaded at Queenie's new house, Bo returned to St. George. He promised to bring Mattie up to visit sometime soon, and he thanked Queenie over and over again for the two fine horses, the cow, the chickens, and the pigs, as well as the furniture and the two boats she had given to him and Mattie.

Queenie and the LaFlours all stayed with Mary and David for a few days while everyone was buying furniture, cleaning up, and arranging both Queenie's house and Genie's little house in the back yard. Mary's cook, Matilda, took Genie home with her each night while they were getting everything in order, and she seemed to take a sincere liking to the little fourteen-year-old girl. For the first time in a long while, Genie was happy. She was thankful to have good food and a comfortable place to sleep, and she could hardly believe that she had her own little house to live in. She was cleaning and scrubbing the place while pieces of furniture were being moved in, and she took great pride in helping Queenie get settled in her new home. Queenie did not have to tell her what to do; Genie just did whatever needed to be done.

While they were working, Queenie asked Genie about her schooling, but Genie did not seem particularly interested. Queenie dropped the subject until they could settle into their new environment, but she felt that Matilda could probably help her convince Genie to attend school. But all that could come later.

When Queenie's house was in fairly good order, the LaFlours returned to St. George. Mary and David continued to be very attentive to Queenie and Genie, and Matilda took Genie to church and saw that she met other little girls her age. Genie was extremely shy, but Matilda felt that time would take care of that problem.

Mary and David took Queenie to church with them. Queenie was nervous at the thought of attending such a large church, but she soon began to recognize people she had known at the Sardis church. After the service, many of her old acquaintances greeted her, and Queenie left that day thinking that the outside was not too bad after all.

As the days passed, Queenie gradually learned to venture to the stores on her own. Sometimes she took Genie along to help carry the groceries home. Genie loved these trips, especially because Queenie sometimes bought her sweets at the grocery store.

"Miss Queenie, we must be rich folks to be buyin' all this good food," Genie said one day as they walked home from the store. "I sure am proud to be workin' for you."

"I'm proud to have you with me, Genie," replied Queenie, "but I want you to get some schoolin'. I've talked with Matilda about this, and she said that her granddaughter, Marty, who is your age, will take you to school with her. I'm goin' to get you some real pretty clothes to wear to school, too."

Genie looked frightened. "Oh, no, Miss Queenie. I just want to stay home and help you."

"You can help me after school and on Saturdays. Now, you know you have to mind me if you want to stay up here in Folkston."

Genie was on the verge of tears. "I know, Miss Queenie, but I'm afraid to go to school. You see, I ain't had no schoolin', not ever. I can't even write my name. The teacher'd put me in the first grade with the little children, and I'll be so ashamed to do that."

"Well, we'll just have to do something about that," replied Queenie. "Beginning today, I'll start teaching you to read and write the best I know how. You see, Genie, I ain't had much education, either. That's why I want you to go to school. Out where we lived, there wasn't any school. My Ma and Pa taught me all they could, but they didn't have much school learnin', either. Now, are you gonna do what I say about this education?"

"Yes'm, I will. I'm sorry I questioned what you told me to do."

The days passed quickly while Queenie adjusted to her new house, with its running water, indoor toilet, and fancy cooking stove. Mary came over to check on her each day and took her shopping in the nearby towns. Eventually, on Mary's advice, Queenie even bought a radio. She and Genie sat for hours listening to the music and the many new programs.

Some of her church friends came to visit her regularly, and Mary took her to church functions during the week. Queenie had learned to enjoy Mary's automobile and was no longer so afraid to ride in it. Mary wrote her mother a long letter describing how well Queenie had adjusted to life in town. Mae was happy to hear this news, because she had been afraid that Queenie, at her age, would never adjust to life on the outside.

Genie proved to be a fast learner, and before long, she agreed to accompany Marty to the black children's school. The teacher soon realized how smart this new student was and placed Genie in a fourth-grade class. There were many other children her own age in her class, so she did not feel as embarrassed as she had feared she might.

Queenie still missed her old home in the south swamp, but each day she was more grateful that she had lived to enjoy the luxuries on the outside. Her chief regret was that her Pa and the others in her family were not able to enjoy the same luxury that she now did. She consoled herself by remembering the happiness they had in their own little world—the hunting, the fishing and quietness, and the beauty of the swamp. The air was so much fresher there. Life was simpler, and the creatures in the Okefenokee seemed somehow closer to God.

Queenie's friend Mary had heard many of the stories of swamp life in the old days. She knew about her Pa's first wife, Dawn, and about their son Joe, who had died during the war in Cuba. She also knew of the Lightfoot family, and she naturally had a keen interest in them, as well as the fact that her Pa's grandson, Will, was related to them.

After one of Mary's friends went to Silver Springs, just below Ocala, Florida, on a vacation, she returned with news that some Indians from the Everglades had camped at this resort during the tourist season. They were selling blankets and other Indian products to the tourists, who, even in the grip of the Depression, somehow continued to flood into Florida. Many of the Indians had found a good market for their products, which they sold to the tourists passing through central Florida on their way to Miami or other cities in south Florida.

When Mary heard of the Indians at Silver Springs, she mentioned them to Queenie. She wondered if any of the Lightfoot family could be among this group. Queenie was immediately interested in this bit of news, and although she realized that the older members of the Lightfoot family would no longer be living, she thought that perhaps some of their descendants might have made their home there. How wonderful it would be to meet some of Pete's children or grandchildren! It had been so long that she dared not hope that Pete himself would still be alive.

Mary promised Queenie that she would talk to David about taking a vacation of their own to Silver Springs. Queenie had never been on such a long trip, but Mary reminded her that Ocala was only about a hundred and fifty miles away, and automobiles now made short work of such distances.

David agreed to take them to Ocala and Silver Springs for a short vacation, but they would have to wait a week or so because he was so busy with his work. The two women became more excited each day, and they spent their time buying new clothes and making plans for the trip.

Matilda agreed to take care of Genie while they were away, and they soon headed south toward Ocala. They registered at the Marion Hotel there, and Queenie believed she had never seen such a beautiful building or so much luxury. They spent several hours sightseeing around Ocala and made plans to drive out to Silver Springs the following day.

Queenie and Mary were up bright and early the next morning, rushing David to take them to Silver Springs. David himself even felt some of their excitement at what they might find there. And even if they did not find any of the Lightfoots, they had heard of the beauty of the area and knew they would enjoy the adventure anyway.

Queenie was nervous. Would they find some of the Lightfoot family? Was there a chance that Pete would be there? How would that once handsome boy look now as an old man? She knew there was very little chance that Pete would be in this part of the state, but she dared to hope that she might at least find someone who could give her news of her friends from so long ago.

When they finally reached Silver Springs, they parked the car and walked over to view the water, the glass-bottomed boats, and the little shops. Queenie, however, was not very interested in these sights. She was instead straining her eyes to see the little Indian encampment in the distance. There were colorful blankets attractively displayed and little children running around everywhere. Most of the adults looked to be busy with the tourist trade. Queenie, Mary, and David walked over to examine the Indian wares. There was much to buy, but Queenie was not looking for blankets and trinkets. She was looking for someone who had features that reminded her of the Lightfoot family. Finally, miraculously, she spied a middle-aged man who bore a remarkable resemblance to Pete Lightfoot. He stood by a little group of Indians who were busy with the sale of their goods. Slowly and deliberately, Queenie walked over and inquired if his name was Lightfoot.

"It is, ma'am," he said, unable to hide his surprise. "Is there something I can do for you?"

"Yes," answered Queenie, a little breathlessly. "You can tell me if you are kin to a man named Pete Lightfoot. You have a great resemblance to him."

"He's my Pa. But he's gettin' on in years, now, so he didn't come up with us this year. Do you know him?"

David and Mary walked up as Queenie answered excitedly that she and Pete were old friends. David introduced himself and his two companions, and he asked the man if he would come and sit with them in the shade and tell them about his family. The man, Jim Lightfoot, first introduced his wife to them, then they all walked to a comfortable place where they could talk.

Jim was a very gracious man and answered the many questions that Queenie asked. He said that his grandparents had been dead for many years and that his father, Pete, was the leader of the Indians in south Florida. His poor health, unfortunately, had recently curtailed his activities. He related that his mother was dead, but Pete had a large family, and his children took good care of him.

"I'll be so glad to tell Pa that I've met you," said Jim. "He's told us so many stories of his life in the Okefenokee. He must have loved all of your family very much. He hoped some day to return to the swamp and visit his friends there, but money is very scarce among our people. Many of our friends and most of our property were lost in the Hurricane of '27. We've never really recovered, and that's the reason we're here at Silver Springs. We need better food and shelter for our people, so we sell as much as we can to the tourists who come along the Tamiami Trail. We do the best we can, but we still need more. Our schools are among the poorest in Florida. The government helps some, but it's not really enough."

Jim knew about Pete's sister, Dawn, and he asked about her husband and son. They told him about Ben's remarriage, about Joe's death in Cuba, and about Joe's son, Will.

Finally, David told their new friend that he knew Jim was needed to help with sales, but seeing the disappointed look on Queenie's face, David promised to return to the Springs for another visit the following day. This was agreeable to everyone, and David then drove them back to their hotel. Queenie was happy to have found Pete's son, but she was left with a feeling of sadness at the realization of how poor they were and how the children needed better schools. Unless they could get an education, she knew that they were doomed to poverty in the Everglades. She discussed her feelings with David and Mary.

"I can't help worryin' about those poor Indian people. I'm wonderin', David, how much money it would take to build a school for those children down there."

"It wouldn't take too much just to build a school," answered David, "but they would have to have enough money to hire teachers, too. That would be their biggest expense. As far as the building itself goes, the people would likely do most of the work themselves if they could get lumber and other supplies. Are you thinkin' of helpin' them, Queenie?"

"Well, we all know that I have money I'll never use. Do you guess there's some way I could go about helpin' them?"

Before David could answer, Mary said, "Oh, Queenie, I think that would be a wonderful thing for you to do!"

"Yes," agreed David. "And it could be done in a businesslike way. If this man, Jim, would agree to supervise the project, you could put your lawyer, James Cook, in charge of supervising the endowment for the school. Why don't you mention this to Jim when we see him tomorrow, and then we can talk with James Cook when we get back to Folkston?"

David was always so level-headed. Queenie wondered what she would do without him and Mary. She wondered as well if her Pa would approve of her spending the Ross money on the education of these Indians. She believed that he probably would, and if David approved, then it must be all right.

They had a nice visit with Jim Lightfoot the following day, and Queenie broached the subject of the school. David explained some of the details of the project and asked Jim if he would be willing to supervise the building of the school. Jim was overwhelmed by the offer. He agreed to supervise the building as well as the organization of the school.

"Now I can see why Pa loves your family so much," laughed Jim. "He told us how your family gave them a horse and wagon to drive to the Everglades." He grew more serious suddenly. "I'm afraid, though, that you might be givin' us money that you need to get by on. Times are still hard all over the country."

"When the government took over our land in the swamp, they paid us for it," answered Queenie. "It wasn't much, but it's more than I'll need. I'm the only one left in our family, and I don't need much. I think my folks would be proud for me to help you all down on the reservation."

"Queenie has a good lawyer in Folkston," added David. "I think he'd handle the financial end of this deal. Of course, she would have to talk this over with him first, but if he thinks he can handle the disbursement of money for building supplies and for hiring teachers, I think this could be worked out rather easily. This lawyer, James Cook, will be in touch with you soon."

David carefully copied down Jim's mailing address, and he and the two women departed the Springs, leaving behind a happy Lightfoot family. David promised to accompany Queenie when she went to talk with James Cook. He and Mary seemed almost as excited as she was about the Indian school. The women could both tell that David was excited, but he cautioned them not to get their hopes up until they talked with James Cook. David warned Queenie not to overspend, since there was no way to predict her own financial needs in the years to come. He knew she was well-off, but he also knew that there was no one else to take care of her. If she lived to be as old as her Pa, she still had quite a bit of time left. He knew that he and Mary would never let her suffer for money, but he knew she would always want to be independent.

The conference with James Cook was very satisfactory. Because Queenie always felt better when she was with Mary, she asked her to go along for support. James Cook thought financing the Indian school was a noble thing for Queenie to do, but he gave her a short lecture, as David had, about holding on to some of her money for later years. Queenie listened and felt that they were giving her unnecessary advice, but she said nothing. She realized that they only had her best interests at heart. The main thing she cared about was getting the deal settled for the school. She was surprised to hear David inform James that he and Mary would also contribute to the school and that he felt certain that his father-in-law would want to do the same. Of course, the bulk of the money would come from Queenie, but they wanted to be a part of this wonderful project, too.

Mary wrote to her parents and told them the news of their trip to Florida and described the plans for the school. Mae wrote that she and Ben were happy with the news and wanted to contribute to the school as well.

Queenie told Genie all about their trip and explained that she hoped to build a school for the Indians in the Everglades. Like everyone else, Genie was excited over the news. She didn't know where the Everglades were, but she even mentioned to Queenie that she might teach in the school some day when she was grown.

"Now, that is a good idea, Genie," said Queenie enthusiastically. "Some day I hope to send you to a college where you can study to be a teacher, and you just might like to teach in that school."

All this talk of money made Queenie consider just how much money she actually had, as well as the fact that she had no plan for what should be done with her estate after she died. She went to see James Cook and described her concerns about how she should dispose of her money and other possessions upon her death. James told her she needed to draw up a will and designate who should benefit from her wealth. She named Mary and David as her beneficiaries, and she left a generous sum for Genie's education, along with a nice amount of money to help Genie get started in life. Queenie requested that this whole arrangement be kept confidential, as long as she was alive.

James assured her that the plans for the Indian school were moving along smoothly, and he promised to keep her informed throughout the progress. Queenie left his office feeling that she had lifted a heavy burden from her shoulders. Now she could put her mind to other things.

James Cook did keep Queenie informed about the progress of the school, and due to the efforts of Jim Lightfoot and the other Indians, the building was completed in a matter of months. Queenie realized how anxious the Indians were to have a school for their children by the speed at which they worked to finish it. Of course, there was the matter of hiring a teacher, but Jim was already working on that. There were some teachers working over in the small towns on the east coast near the Tamiami Trail, and Jim was able to convince some of them to come over and conduct classes on Saturdays until a permanent teacher could be hired.

Jim wrote to Queenie, describing how the school was nearing completion and how much all of his people appreciated what she had done. Queenie felt very satisfied that she had done something really worthwhile for them. She remembered the Lightfoot family and how much they had meant to her and her family so many years ago. Somehow, she just knew that her parents and grandparents would be pleased with what she had done. With the donations from the LaFlours and Mary and David, there had been plenty of money to build a modern school and adequately furnish it, as well.

A few weeks later, James Cook received a letter from Jim Lightfoot informing him that the school was completed and that they were planning a celebration for its grand opening. Jim hoped that Mr. Cook would be able to attend this celebration and enclosed another letter for Queenie. James carried it right over to Queenie and waited while she read it. After Queenie read the letter, she gave it to James. She could not believe its contents. It was an invitation for Miss Queen Ross and her friends to attend the opening of the Ross

Indian School in about two weeks. Jim was pleased to inform her that they were honored to name the school after Miss Ross, who had so graciously provided money for the school. The Indians especially hoped that the other people who had made contributions would be able to come, and Jim asked that she inform him if she and any of her friends would be able to attend the celebration.

James watched as big tears rolled down Queenie's cheeks. "Will you be able to attend, Mr. Cook?" she asked.

"I do wish I could, Miss Ross," he answered, "but I have an important court case up at Waycross at that time. But I think that David and Mary will want to go. I certainly hope all three of you will be able to attend the celebration."

When James Cook left, Queenie just sat quietly for a few minutes. She was shaking from the excitement, and she just could not believe that this was actually happening! As soon as she calmed herself sufficiently, she walked briskly over to Mary's house. No words would come, so she simply handed the letter to Mary. After reading it, Mary called to David, who was in the back part of the house. She handed the letter to him, and he quickly read it and then hugged both women. "Go out tomorrow and get yourselves a new dress, ladies!" he said. "We'll soon be headin' for Miami and the new Ross School!"

Both women hugged each other and literally danced around the room. After they quieted down a little, Mary said, "That's a long ride, Queenie. Are you sure you're up to the trip?"

"Oh, I'm fine, Mary. But do you think Ben and Mae will be able to go?"

"I doubt it, but I'll write them tonight and see if they think they can make the trip. Oh, they'll be so happy to hear this good news!"

"David, you're the kindest man in the world," said Queenie. "What would we do without you?"

"Well, Queenie, I hope you never have to find out. I'm happy to make this trip with you, and I know we're going to have a good time."

Mary and Queenie did buy new dresses, as well as new hats for the trip. Ben and Mae thought the trip would be a little too much for them, but they both expressed their happiness about the new school and the upcoming celebration.

After days of shopping and planning, Queenie and her friends were finally ready to leave for Miami. Not only were they pleased about the celebration, but they were excited about this trip as well. Mary and David had been to Jacksonville and other cities in north Florida many times, but this was their first trip to Miami. Queenie, of course, had never been to any town larger than Ocala. She was excited and a little afraid that she would not know how to act in such a large city. She voiced her concern to Mary, but Mary assured her that David would know what to do and would take care of them. Queenie knew Mary was right, and she felt reassured.

Finally the departure day arrived. Queenie left Genie in Matilda's safe hands, and she felt that she didn't have a worry in the world. They piled into David's comfortable car, and before too long, they had left Georgia behind and were traveling toward Jacksonville. Queenie could not believe her eyes when they passed through the city. She settled back to enjoy the beautiful scenery they were passing, and she leaned her head on the back of the seat and closed her eyes. She must now get her thoughts together. She must remember all the things she had planned to tell Pete when she saw him. She must tell him all about Grandma and Grandpa, and about his nephew, Little Joe, and Joe's son, Will. She must tell him about Ma and Pa, and how Pa had lived to be such an old man, and how the government had taken the swamp under its control, and how she had moved to Folkston to live. How glad she would be to tell him that Ben was still living and that his fine wife, Mae, was also well!

Mary looked back at Queenie and asked softly, "Are you awake, Queenie? You've gotten so quiet that I thought you must be asleep."

"No, Mary, I'm not asleep," replied Queenie. "I was just rememberin'. I can't seem to get straight in my mind all that I want to tell Pete when I see him. I hope he'll be able to tell me all about his family and what's happened to them through the years."

"I hope so, too," said Mary, and she turned to gaze quietly out the window.

As Queenie laid her head back once more and closed her eyes, she whispered softly to herself. "It's been so long! There's so much to remember, so very much to remember!"